The Search
for an
Inappropriate Man

The Search for an Inappropriate Man

Stories

RoseMarie London

iUniverse, Inc.
New York   Lincoln   Shanghai

The Search for an Inappropriate Man
Stories

iUniverse books may be ordered through booksellers or by contacting:

iUniverse
2021 Pine Lake Road, Suite 100
Lincoln, NE 68512
www.iuniverse.com
1-800-Authors (1-800-288-4677)

ISBN-13: 978-0-595-35754-3 (pbk)
ISBN-13: 978-0-595-80231-9 (ebk)
ISBN-10: 0-595-35754-7 (pbk)
ISBN-10: 0-595-80231-1 (ebk)

Printed in the United States of America

For Mom
the wind beneath my wings

And in memory of
George Basil Aridas

Acknowledgments

The author would like to thank the following institutions for their support: The Ucross Foundation and the Wyoming Arts Council. "Commerce" was published as "Nina and Luke" in *Profligate Desire*; "In Ranch Country Men are Valued by their Ability with Horses" was published in *Anthology One*, the Alsop Review Press; "The Scientologist with Situational Ethics" was published in *Facsimilation Magazine*; "The Woodworker from Long Island" was published in *ElevenBulls*; "Three Day Expedite" was published in *Del Sol Review* and reprinted in *Carve Magazine*; "Red, Blue and the WWE" was published in *Matter Journal*; "Office Affair" was published by *Small Spiral Notebook*; "On Being Misidentified" was published in a slightly different form in *Prose Toad*; "Life at the Club" was published as "Cocktailing Cliches" in *Dicey Brown*.

Natasha

Patterns

I'd lived in Wyoming for five years before I got shot standing beside the wrong man at the wrong time next to a pool table in a bar where, up to that moment, it looked as though I was going to walk away from a win that would clear my tab.

It was some crime of passion—not mine—I paid for with a bullet through the shoulder. In my estimation it probably makes up for all the passionate misdeeds I'd gotten away with. Karma's funny that way, it seems.

I don't remember the commotion that followed the through and through. There was less blood and less pain than I would have otherwise thought. And I didn't fall right away to the ground. Women are always in pain; I perpetually experienced a tightness in my chest, or what felt like a fist between my shoulder blades, or a stitch in my side to follow some thought or another I shouldn't have been thinking. The fist. I thought that's all it was.

3

I'd just been talking with a good looking student pastor while waiting for a bourbon refill. He was sitting alone, reading a book I'd read, and drinking the same color drink as I. Simpatico enough in a small town. He happened to say that he thought he was about to get fired—not uncommon bar conversation. Turned out he was considered a fine shepherd but less of a recruiter than his ministry would like. While I waited for my turn at the table, we began to talk about faith. Or lack of faith. Or being luke-warm, to tell the truth. He told me that a woman whom he had been dating was soon off to Brazil and had asked him to email her every once in a while. "It's what a man would say," he said. "I want something assertive, aggressive even. I will not email her *every once in a while*. I deserve better than luke-warm," he said.

"Is God in Brazil, you think?" I asked. I stared quite decidedly between his legs for a moment. I wanted to get him in the bathroom, strip him of his pressed jeans and crisp Carhartt and fuck him aggressively. Instead, I responded to the crack of one pool ball against another.

"I'm Tom," he said as I was about to go.

I think Tom was the one to call an ambulance. He sent me a basket of fruit and a paperback edition Old Testament with Psalm 51 marked. Dark stuff, that.

I was a cheater. I learned from the best. My few attempts at monogamy have invariably failed. I never got better at it, only at cheating. I'd been cheating on my boyfriend when I got shot. Well, not at that exact moment. But consistently for about a year with one particular man.

I was at that bar to get away from both of them. It was way, way out of town. And I was playing pool with a bunch of guys I knew only by two or three degrees of separation, which is intimate enough for a game of stick in a bar in the middle of fucking no where.

The guys, all friends of Tuck, with whom I'd arrived at the bar in his F-350 Diesel, were all making fun of my fancy boots, calling me the Dog, that bounty hunter who has his own show on cable. My D cups in the merino wool turtle neck however, rendered them speechless. Bottom line is that I'm a big city girl and so it was the three hundred dollar stitched boots in the window of the western store across the street from the town bar with the neon bucking horse that attracted me and thus all manner of derisive comment.

Tuck walked with a limp from a bad accident that made him a Ford man and swore him off GMC's for good which is why we left my truck at the Holiday Inn in town and took his out into the dark. Tuck's strong shoulders caught my eye all night the same way the preacher man's sitting position did. The way some admire fine art that traveled around the world from museum to museum, I admire the architecture of a man.

Clearly I had not been the only one admiring Tuck lately. My bullet, a 9mm gifted from a broken-hearted husband with a Smith and Wesson, had been meant for him. I'd just made the winning shot and backed up too soon and took one in the shoulder for him. That boy Tuck sure did have luck on his side. Must have replaced his manners because I've not had one message from him since.

After the ambulance, the emergency room, the sling—my drinking arm will never be the same for sure—I left Wyoming and went just about to Mexico in search of my one true love. The whole luke-warm thing at the bar that night got me doing some hospital bed thinking about Jim, the one I let get away. I'd heard he'd put his name on a Harley dealership and that he still loved his Jack Daniels. Jim could still tug at me, and neither he nor I were getting any younger.

When I find him he's with someone but details like that don't matter to someone who's been shot at. And when I find him, I'm still significantly worked up by all the crap I had to read while searching for news of him on the world wide web. Trash talk, threads I think they're called, from a bunch of lonely, nobody, loser wanna-be's in chat rooms related to the band Jim used to be in. It just about killed me, all the bullshit I had to wade through to catch myself up on him.

It wasn't so much all the girls talking, girls from places like Detroit or Florida, with their innuendos and emoticons hoping to attract attention. No, it was the dude who claimed to have been drinking beer, joy riding in Jim's truck with him through the Arizona wild-fires last summer. That one got me. Gave me a pain worse than that bullet.

I found Jim bowling. I wanted him to be the one who saw me, so for a long time I stayed at the bar beside the shoe kiosk, drinking four-dollar Beam and Cokes out of Dixie cups. Drinks that were more muddy-tasting ice than anything; it took three. I kept watch, though focused on noises coming from my stomach.

Though the alley was dirty and dark, with one old fixture flashing green, red and blue lights, I would have known Jim was there even if I hadn't spotted him as soon as I came in. The whole place could hear him laugh and shout. He was wearing tight fitting blue jeans and a red and yellow bowling shirt, which I already knew had a tipped martini glass with a pimento stuffed olive embroidered on it alongside his name; he had on his own bowling shoes—blue sparkled like an early seventies Nova—and inside his bowling bag there were two more pair with their custom heels and a special rag to wipe them clean. Jim and I used to bowl; I was getting good at it too.

It was noon and people began to fill the cafeteria like it was somewhere special to eat. And then it happened. Jim upended a bottle of Corona and turned his gaze to plot his way to the bar. Foam dripped suggestively from the tapered end of the bottle while Jim took a moment to convince himself of me. Then he smiled, I'd like to think. I can't be sure. Though ill advised, I'd been wearing the same pair of disposable contacts for weeks and I had some serious floaters.

I paid for his next beer, squared my shoulders in the bandana halter top I had on, and walked it on over.

"Hey lover," I said.

"Who the fuck shot you?" Jim said, poking the pucker of what was once a hole.

"You don't know him."

Remember a while back when Lists were all the rage. Everyone was a list maker. Even I got one published in *McSweeney's* and then immediately regretted it, even though I'm sure no one I know ever saw it. Well, let me stop here a moment to list a few things that might describe how unlike me the current girlfriend, who was standing beside him, was.

She's Cover Girl Pink, I'm Laura Mercier Sienna.

She's Candies and I'm Donald Pliner.

She's a-gasp!-Stripper I can type ninety words a minute and construct decent sentences.

Ok, my summary preference for men over women has never been a secret. And women who are standing in my way rank even lower. Needless to say I ignored her and her proximity to the man, whom if the itchy feeling under my arms was any indication, I was still in love with.

"Break 280 yet?" I said.

"Long time ago."

Until then, Jim's girlfriend had been in a sort of stunned trance that I wasn't convinced didn't come naturally. Suddenly she began puffing furiously on her cigarette, her left hand supporting her right elbow. And then inexplicably, she turned on her plastic mold heel and was swallowed up by the smog and lingering kitchen grease. Hopefully for good, though I doubted it.

"I think Barbie's upset," I said.

"Wouldn't be the first time," Jim said. He snapped closed a Zippo and pushed it into his pocket. "And her name's Kimmy. You might say it a few times to remember. I know how good you are with names."

"Kimmy. Barbie. I bet she'd answer to either."

"I've missed you, Tash."

"I'm using the full on Natasha these days, ok."

"Good to know." Jim took four rhythmic steps and let loose the ball. Gutter. "So, where've you been?" he said.

"Wyoming."

"Whiskey's cheap there, I hear."

"Sure is."

"Cold and windy, though."

"That's why the whiskey's cheap."

By this time Kimmy returned all skips and smiles that the sight of me immediately deflated.

"I'm still here," I said. "And I'm staying."

Jim laughed. With my good shoulder I shrugged off the slight; twice before I'd left him.

"Jim," Kimmy pleaded. Just like a child, I tell you. With a precocious little cock to her head and, if I didn't know better, a stamping foot.

"What?" Jim was finding all this endlessly amusing. "What? When I woke up this morning, do you think I knew Tash—I mean, Na Ta Sha," he corrected deliberately, "was going to waltz through the door?"

"Well," Kimmy said. "Who is she?"

"Natasha," Jim said, taking off toward the out of bounds line. I would bet in the tone of Jim's voice Kimmy heard her life crashing like all ten of those pins. On second thought, was she that smart? I'd find out.

I planted myself on the bench behind the electronic scoring do-dad, and rummaged through Jim's bowling bag for a new pack of cigarettes. I'd quit, but now was as good a time as ever to start again.

When Jim found the Bible under the truck seat along with a couple empty Starbucks Mocha Frappuccino bottles and wads of chewed gum, he didn't say anything. He didn't have to. The look on his face was enough. An old can of Copenhagen I had no idea was there, now that made him chatty.

I said, "What the fuck are you doing under the seat anyway?"

Jim'd told Kimmy to go home, that he'd see her in a couple of days. Me personally, I couldn't figure why she'd gotten so upset, it was after all Jim's place she'd been banished to.

"So are you going to tell me about this Bible, Tash?"

"Careful Jim, I might just read it to you!"

"No you won't."

One of the reasons, though not the biggest reason, I kept walking out on Jim was that he didn't own one book. Not one. I watched him stare at the novel I'd left on the coffee table the first time I was living with him. I watched him circle it like it was a rattler. Maybe Jim might read take out menus and he once preferred that I read his band's itinerary for him. To him. But even that he wanted abridged.

"Just don't tell me you got shot and Found God, Tash."

"Nope. But I hear He's in Brazil."

"What?"

"Would you please drive, Jim," I said yanking us to the curb, hitting the hazzards. "I don't know where the fuck I'm going."

"Sure-shit ain't gonna be Brazil."

Jim and I ended up at this kitschy place outside of Bisbee called Shady Dell that rented out vintage Airstreams and the like to crash in. Jim paid the tab for a ten footer built from a Popular Mechanic's blue print in 1952 and decorated in a mid-century southwest motif. I thought it was sweet that he remembered how much I liked a Roy Rogers theme. We drove to the nearest Circle K and stocked up on condoms, junk food and booze. I was gnawing on a strawberry Twizzlers the whole way back to the park.

The bed was barely that, not that it mattered; Jim and I rarely, if ever, fucked in bed.

"Jim," I said, turning my face against the pillow, leaving some drool that was pink from the candy. "Remember the last time I left?"

"Mmm," he said. He was laying on his back, smoking a cigarette; he had his eyes closed. I could feel the heat of his exertion wafting off of him still.

"I made a deal with the devil that night that if I could just survive leaving you that I wouldn't ask too much of anything or anyone anymore, as if I ever had. My point is," I said raising on one elbow, stopping to pick something out of a molar that even after examination I couldn't classify. "My point is, that when I was lying in a hospital bed with an unnatural hole through my body, that was when I should have been making deals with the devil, you know? But, I'd already used up my chance. On you.

"There's something else Jim. I've been spending my life going by the rules I lived when I was with you. And you just can't live that way in the real world. You can't even talk about it."

Jim had his eyes open now. "Morality is the herd instinct in the individual," he said.

I looked at him. I pulled myself back aways to get a better view. "I don't think I even want to know where you heard that."

We were both quiet for a while.

Jim said, "It's hard for me to hear that I am some sort of a go/no go for you."

"I'm not asking you to." I crossed my arms under my boobs and shoved them back where they belonged. "It's not your catastrophe."

"Oh sweetheart, you're much too good for me. You know I can only forget that that's the case for short periods of time."

Jim went home to Kimmy, as I knew he would. She eventually left him for someone with a bigger dealership, as predictable as that is. I managed to get to Brazil. I had a few tropical drinks and came home. I am still single. I think back on Shady Dell and would like to believe that it isn't likely that I would see Jim again at some point down the line. I said, I'd like to believe that. I do know that in spite of all my strengths, and there are new ones popping up all the time, there is something tremendous I'm supposed to learn from it all. But I stopped believing that bullshit that everything happens for a reason the night I got shot. That said, I can't begin to know what the fuck the lesson is.

Anna

Life at the Club

Between her seventeenth and eighteenth years, Anna scored a job cocktailing at a notorious rock club in Queens where she used to go when it was a roller rink and she was four or five years younger. It was while she was cocktailing there that she got into the one and only true car accident she'd ever been in. On her way to work, the gypsy cab driver lost track of the street and crashed into a walk/don't walk pole on the median. Anna cracked her head on the plexiglass partition, but not too hard.

"I'm all right," she said, checking her forehead for blood. "Just keep going."

She held back however, her otherwise generous tip.

The club was devoid of ambience, but it was the biggest room around, and for that reason attracted all the national acts. Anna's first night of work, the place was full to capacity with disciples of the Gregg Allman band. By last call, Anna felt sticky with all the tequila sunrises and shots of Southern

Comfort she'd hoofed around. Anna was pleased to find that picking through a crush of rubbery drunks while holding a drinks tray over your head wasn't as hard as it might have been. Anna's balance was excellent in her five-inch stilettos: tuck your ass in, center your shoulders over your hips and you are not likely to have any trouble. Still, she watched with curious apprehension as it took almost until the next night for her toes to turn from purple back to pink.

Some of the waitresses had been working there from the very first and were understandably territorial. Some of them had little stuffed animals or other identifying brick-a-brack glued to their trays, so that their regulars could recognize them from the tray over their heads when they were otherwise entirely hidden from view. Anna thought that was a pretty snappy idea, but was not a stuffed animal kind of girl. She had no loyalty to certain ball point pens either. She kept her tray clear, and didn't throw a methadone like fit when it turned up missing the next time she came to work and was left to use the one that was cracked and therefore bound to topple drinks.

The owners of the club were third or fourth tier Mafiosa, all black polyester, twenty-four carat gold and Brill Creamed hair. The top floor, a space above the concession area that must have always smelled like the same six kielbasa that jerked around in the rotisserie every night, was rumored to house their poorly-run brothel. The cocktail waitresses were not allowed to sit down during their seven p.m. to four a.m. shift, and so Anna was rarely ever near the concession long enough to catch anyone heading up the stairs that she'd heard were behind an oddly situated emergency exit.

Since having to pee was the only excuse to sit, the toilet seat cover dispenser in the bathroom was always empty. The waitresses would lift handfuls of them from the diner up the block at breakfast and stash them in their purses the way old ladies took the packets of sugar and individual servings of grape jelly. And since you were required to leave your stuff with everyone else's beside the rusty sink pipes under the unlocked bathroom vanity, toilet seat covers, like other essential wares such as hairspray, tampons and ball point pens, were fair game. After the owner hired a physically challenged bathroom attendant whose sole purpose was to rat out lazy waitresses, life at the club was survival of the fittest.

Waitresses began buying the Down's Syndrome attendant's silence with hard candy and brightly colored hair accessories, so sometimes there might be three waitresses in the ladies' room at once, the most diabolical of the group having sweet talked the unsteady attendant out of her folding chair.

In a room with a fire department capacity of five-thousand, even the non-national act nights were hard, dangerous work. As a novice cocktail waitress, Anna had been relegated to the floor area only, while other waitresses had two drink minimum sections and the floor. It was dog-eat-dog. One weekend, one of the waitresses was reported MIA and at the last minute Anna was reluctantly assigned her section by one of the Members Only jacket wearing owners.

"Stay on ya toes, hear? I don't want dis section to get a bad rep," he told her.

It was the middle of February and Anna hoped that working a carpeted section, three feet off the floor, might be warmer than the concrete floor. The monolith HVAC units hung from dusty chains in all four corners of the space, silent and irrelevant; the owners never turned them on.

Eventually Anna was allowed to work the VIP section but on a regular, meaning non-national act night, and made fourteen dollars in tips, seven of which at the end of the night had to be offered to the service bartender. It would have been thirty four, but she'd handed back the extra twenty that she'd been given by mistake. It occurred to Anna that balance notwithstanding, she might not have the mettle for this line of work.

On President's Day weekend, in the middle of a freak storm, the line to get into the club to see Queensryche wrapped around the block. The owners opened late so they could joke about the stupid fanaticism of the denim and leather crowd left standing out in the snow. The wanna-be gangster cousins packed them in that night, eight-thousand strong. Not long before the act went on, the waitresses were trapped by the service bar in the space below the dee jay.

From the top of a broken chair, Anna watched the crowd rippling like surf. There was evidence of shouting, blood; the air smelled sour with adrenaline. So that none of the staff could sneak friends in through the parking lot, the alternate exit doors behind her were, as they always were, chained shut.

Anna figured all bets were off and climbed over the back of the chair and up into the dee jay's crows nest. Still Anna crouched below the booth window, balancing on her tall heels, ass not touching the floor, so no one would see she was there.

"Something bad is definitely going to happen," the skinny dee jay said. His long hair dangling down his back, a cigarette loose in his mouth, he squeezed one half of his headset between ear and shoulder expertly dropping the stylus on a record.

"Did you remember to take your lithium tonight?" Anna asked.

"Here," the dee jay reached for something in the dark and tossed Anna a collapsible umbrella. "Can you hold that over my turntables? It's starting to rain."

Anna hadn't noticed the thick globs of water—murky condensation from the heat and breath of the bursting crowd—that had accumulated on the ceiling.

"I've been watching this barometric anomaly for the last twenty minutes or so," he said.

One Saturday evening in June, Anna met the waitresses outside on the sidewalk. Yellow crime scene tape circled the perimeter of the building.

"What happened?" Anna asked.

"Some kid got beat to death last night. They found him in the dumpster over there." Delila, the most senior of the service staff waved her cigarette toward the narrow alley separating the club from the Magic Carpet Discount Warehouse next door.

Anna found herself absorbed, not by the news—no, that didn't seem to surprise anyone—but by the faces in the waning daylight of the women with whom she'd worked for a year.

"I guess the party's over," Dee said.

As though having just been given permission, the waitresses stubbed out lipstick stained Parliaments with disaffected shrugs and began to filter away.

"Anna," Dee said. "I heard that one of the girls who sits on a swing over the bar at the Limelight's about to quit." Dee looked Anna up and down. "You'd be good for that."

The Woodworker
from Long Island

It is Christmas-time and they arrange to meet on a thirty-degree Friday night in front of the Tree. This is Jason's idea, this first date kitsch, and Anna knows that she will have to circuit Rockefeller Plaza to find him standing where he considers in front of the Tree to be.

Jason lives with a roommate in a one-bedroom, mother part of a mother/daughter mortgaged to his parents. During the day, he works with wood at Creative Kitchen in Bayshore. Before leaving Penn Station, Jason buys Anna a rose. It suffocates in hard cellophane. The stem is squeezed by a plastic Santa.

Jason pays for dinner with cash. Later Anna learns it is the money his mother has given him to supplement his Christmas shopping. Woodworking, does not pay well.

Love Shack, Baby.

Jason drives fifty-two miles through an icy rain in a '74 Beetle with no heat to pick Anna up for their second date. It is New Year's Eve. East on the LIE, he vigorously rubs her thigh to keep her warm. Anna is less concerned with hypothermia than she is with the tin-can construction of the car.

Jason takes her to a neighborhood with no sidewalks and few street lights. There are plastic reindeer on the front lawn, beer in an ice-filled avocado-green American Standard bath tub and two six-foot subs spanning the kitchen sink. Jason is the life of the party so there is some commotion when he arrives.

Jason's friends are kind enough, more curious of Anna than invested.

MTV supplants Dick Clark and after the countdown and the confetti, the first video of 1991 is *Love Shack*. The particular way he kisses her at midnight confirms the wisdom of what has been the unlikely decision to stand some of her friends up in Tribeca.

When Anna gets back in the Bug, there is a stuffed animal on her seat. Anna has never received silly courtship gifts before and becomes momentarily overwhelmed.

"I thought we'd go back to my place," Jason says.

"Don't you have a roommate?"

"He sleeps on the couch."

"Does he get a discount in rent?"

"Yes, actually."

The animal sits in her lap as he drives. She smokes a cigarette over its head.

The door to his apartment is in the back yard and is kept unlocked. There is a path of landscape lights to follow. He takes her hand and brings her past a shadowy heap on a sofa bed to the bedroom. Anna's heels clap against the linoleum. Jason closes the hollow-core door behind him. There is a mattress on the floor. Anna hears the whisper of his clothes and a click. An electric blanket dial glows orange in the dark. The cord disappears between the mattress and the sheet. The baseboard heating costs too much to run.

Jason's body is sinewy. Anna's fingers find grooves that in the light she will discover are traces of growing pains. She is less quiet than he, but right before he comes Jason warns, "I'm gonna squirt." He seems shocked. Anna is a little horrified by his word choice.

Jason's New Girlfriend

As Jason's new girlfriend, Anna becomes one of those weekend travelers who clog the great room of Penn Station on Friday nights. It's all a surprise to her. She rides the Babylon line, the only one not flashing the conductor a monthly ticket with a patent look of exhaustion and inconvenience.

Massapequa, Massapequa Park, Amityville, Copaigue, Lindenhurst, the conductor says. It is the melody and not the word which prompts Anna to rise, slide out of the row and ride the gentle rocking in front of the doors. She watches her reflection in the glass, and the people behind her.

Jason will be waiting under the platform at the foot of the stairs, inside the Beetle which will be enveloped in white exhaust. One Friday night he presents her with a wooden sculpture of a dinosaur, laminated like counter-top. The gift comes in two-parts. Herbivore and a dialog bubble that reads: you make me feel *primative*.

Sunday Macs with the Parents

Jason brings Anna home for dinner. There is a cloying mix of tomato sauce on simmer and steam seeping through the vents of a perpetually cooling dishwasher. Anna climbs a few stairs and meet Jason's parents in the kitchen. Jason's father stands, slips out from behind the table to greet her. Jason's mother wipes her hands on a terry cloth apron to watch.

Halfway through the ziti, his mother puts down her fork.

"She's not at all like Trisha, Jason." Her small fingers are curled into her palms, her wrists rest on the edge of the table, the heat from her dish adds more color to her face.

"Ma," Jason says.

"I miss her Jason. What can I tell you?"

"Pardon me," Anna says. "Who's Trisha?"

"Trisha was my girlfriend for eight years," Jason says to her.

"She was only here two weeks ago, Jason."

"Ma, we broke up. She's not dead."

"It's just, you two have broken up before and you've never done this."

"This?" Not-Trisha says.

"This?" Jason says too.

"Selina, stop it," Jason's father says and then turns to Anna. "This must be very uncomfortable for you. I guess what my wife is afraid of, well, they were very well suited, Trisha and Jason. And you, well, are you here to see how the other half lives?"

Anna chokes. "The other half?"

"We're very proud of Jason," his father says. "Don't misunderstand me. But, aren't you casting your line in the wrong pond?"

Spit

They go to Spit to drink and sometimes dance wildly. They come home drunk, taking back roads, avoiding the cops. They have sloppy sex. Parts of them are embarrassingly stuck together in the morning. And at dusk, they stop at IHOP to feed the hangovers made by Rumple Minz, his, and Fuzzy Navels, hers, before Jason drives Anna back to the City.

It takes a whole month of dirty dancing at Spit—where sometimes Anna thinks she sees her ex-boyfriend Eric, the one who died of cancer—for her to realize that the point where Jason slows down on the back route, across disused train tracks and over some marshy spots, is beneath the window of Trisha's apartment.

When Anna realizes it, she doesn't say anything. But Jason surprises her at the 7-Eleven one night on the way to Spit, when he stops for a pack of cigarettes, he donates a dollar to the Muscular Dystrophy Association and fills out a paper heart in his and Anna's name which hangs over the beer case well past Mother's Day. It is the 7-Eleven nearest Trisha's window.

Three Day Expedite

What's in a name?

For the longest time Anna didn't know his name, while he knew that she got her linens from the Company Store—slept in a queen-size bed—and, with some consistency, ordered from J. Crew and less frequently, from Victoria's Secret. Knowing his name was as easy as just asking. He might have even told her once. It is something with two syllables.

One day Anna found herself dogging him.

She had started saving up her dry cleaning and other car-necessary errands all week for one afternoon where she might come across him standing behind his truck. Anna never strayed too far out of her way looking, maybe just a block more this way or that.

One day things were different. Anna saw the top of a brown truck at the crest of a hill. The light changed and it drove on past where she would otherwise make a turn.

Before she knew it, she was through the light too and weaving across the double yellow for a peek, even though from behind like this, Anna couldn't be sure that it was him.

Anna's heart was racing along with her engine. Humming with the air-conditioning. No sooner did she tell herself she would go no further than the elementary school, the truck made a right and Anna raced through a stop sign and sped around two corners to cut it off.

Anna found the truck hugging a curb, and catching sight of him in his Bermuda shorts, undetected, satisfied her secret game of tag. Anna was pleased and went home and mixed a pitcher of lemonade to pour into some vodka.

Anna ordered two white Jersey cap-sleeve deep V-neck t-shirts, item no. 52179, from J. Crew and waited a few days.

She showered early, made a pot of coffee and sat with a clear view of the street through the storm door. Anna was still working on her first cup as he came up the brick steps.

"No, let me. The box is dirty."

Anna let him in and handed him a steaming cup. He stood with an elbow propped on the back of one of the tall dining room chairs that she had inherited. "French roast," he said.

There was a runny tattoo on his forearm. Anna couldn't help but ask, and he offered the story about his getting the Raging Bull call while at the pizza place in the nearby strip mall, and the fifteen Iraqis who were one minute smoking cigarettes, lying about their tank like mountain sheep, and the next were just a spark and a puff in the dark, Arabian night.

I wish I weren't wearing this bulky sweater, Anna thought.

"I'd better be off. I'll just talk and talk if you let me," he told her carrying his cup to the sink. Running it under the tap. Henry. The tattoo read HENRY.

Anna guessed it was like that song: In the desert, you can't remember your name.

Salami on white.

"Hey, baby!" he said, in his slow got nothing to lose way. He was in the street, his back to traffic, stacking boxes on a hand truck. It was drizzling. "What are you doin' out in the rain?"

"Playing hooky," Anna said.

Henry looked at his wrist. "I take lunch in ten minutes. Should I come by?"

"Sure. Sure," Anna smiled. "Come on by."

Anna's dog sniffed around his ankles and knees. Henry took a seat at the table where she'd laid out two place mats and patted the animal's head. "She must smell my dog."

"You have a dog?"

"A Maltese Poodle."

A can of soda exploded over Anna's hand. He's married. Anna was about to say, that sounds like the kind of dog a man inherits, when Henry stood and asked if he could wash up.

Her loyal pet followed him and Anna listened to him wooing her over a rush of water and thought of all the dirty soap sluicing down between his fingers.

Anna thought about the truck parked at a hydrant in front of the house next door on an otherwise quiet one-way street and how it would stay there, crushing the drooping limbs of the neighbor's cherished birch tree, for longer than it takes to collect a signature.

Henry unfurled a brown bag lunch of salami and Wonder bread. "So, what are you going to do this weekend?"

That's a slightly different question than what are you doing this weekend, and Anna took a moment. She didn't know anymore what she might want to do other than except maybe curl up on the couch with a good book and a bottle of wine.

"Do you go out?" he tried again.

"Not much. I've been working on my Master's thesis on book preservation."

This was a lie.

"What, you mean, like a librarian?"

Henry had his sleeves rolled up in messy curls and Anna could see his watch. The hour was winding down. The dog was restless; she had to chase her around a bit to get her to behave.

Anna began absently pruning dead leaves off a nearby philodendron. Henry pushed his chair back.

It wasn't all her fault. Henry had proved too easy to classify. Ten minutes in and she knew. She knew before he could tell her what kind of car he drove, and from what neighborhood he came, and maybe even what kind of underwear he wore. And I'd been intrigued enough to have hunted him? she said to herself. How had that happened? She wouldn't think about it. It just had.

Walking. Talking. Falling.

Steadily east in a straight line, busy searching left and right at every intersection for any trace; Anna dislikes the exercise.

Listening for an exhaust note which might provide a sighting. Each step getting closer and further. Her chances are dwindling and it feels like she is being squeezed into the vanishing point ahead. Anna's disappointment builds upon itself until it is bigger than she can carry. She trips on uneven concrete. Missteps actually. She begins to think about a strong drink. She can taste the sour cold already.

She turns the key but she knows she is going back out, this time with the car to look more places, faster. Anna twines a long scarf a few times around her neck and changes out of heels. The steering wheel is cold. It is nearly dark. She goes back the way she came and corners into a parking lot where she once saw him drive past. There are X marks like this one all over her subconscious.

I need a few things, Anna surmised. I could go into the grocery and fill a basket to make a good show to myself.

Anna's thinking this when one of those brown trucks gets caught in her side-view. She hears the driver's door roll open and there he is. Standing just across the street. Under a lamp that has just sensed the dusk.

Anna waits for Henry to see her.

He finds Anna's distress amusing, makes fun, pretends to hide their faces behind a corrugated cardboard box that he is holding in one hand way up high in all its bulk, like an acrobat practiced at negotiating awkward props for an audience.

They disagree on where to meet. In ten minutes; on this they consent. By then it would just so happen to be dark.

Anna slips into the store past the deli man who'd been on the sidewalk and was witness to their exchange. He is laughing at her, wiggling behind his food-smeared smock.

Anna gathers random produce into her arms, not checking for rot, and pays in haste, crumpling bills into her jacket pocket. Later when she washes the red tipped lettuce leaf-by-leaf, caressing the soft veins before pulling it to pieces, and later still when the leaves drip olive oil from her fork, it will be Henry velvet in her mouth.

Anna shuts the engine and collapses the lights to wait. She looks away when he pulls up behind her and unlocks the door blindly waiting for him to get in.

Henry tells her to move the car away from the corner. With him in her car with her, a controlled sense of proportion begins to slip. Reality is elastic and Anna is stretching it thin. At some point it will recoil and sting her.

Henry yawns. "I'm bored." It is sport after all.

Ann laughs at her own surprise when she pulls him out of his company issue pants. She is both hungry and frightened and sees the end to this road coming fast and does not care. He reeked of a man interested only in what was convenient and the idea of being or not being in this category petrified her in equal measure.

For the love of country.

When two days later Henry and Anna walk on the dark side of a street to an anonymous bar and he holds out his arm for her to take, Anna feels deliciously small.

And then there is the Desert Storm jacket with his embroidered name and the wash of testosterone when strangers want to shake his heroic hand as he passes them on his way to pee.

Anna smelled the Newports on him on Christmas Eve when he was leaning against her fridge. She was elbow deep in ingredients for a feast and he was dripping city snow on her newly-mopped floor. When he took the cellophane package (MarthaStewart.com) of home-baked sugar cookies out of her hand and asked her if she'd let him hang her upside-down, she could taste it.

Henry takes an empty pack of cigarettes from his pocket and tosses them beside the change on the bar. Somewhere in the back of his mind, Anna's Gulf War hero knows that his opportunities are shrinking and that he will never be a rich man by any means. He works hard and swallows down with a permanent smile what he feels is his unique list of unrealized dreams. He is dutiful to a point to his unhappy or oblivious wife and each week prepares a grand Sunday dinner with his little girl who, he says, sweetly resembles him in all her pre-teen awkwardness. A third of the way into a mortgage on a house that's just a little too small and a little too close to the ones beside it, at thirty-nine he's all about his things: the medals and certificates on display in his den, the hunting cabin he shares with two beat cops and a tricked out Grand Prix that's irritatingly temperamental and never really runs right. Anna knows this man. She remembers when, like his daughter now, she was eleven and it was her father collecting things that eased his disappointments.

Anna laughs at the sight of herself in the mirror over the bar back, so entirely out of her habitat, singing in her head, "I love a man in a uniform." But she accepts a drink on the house for the love of country.

Anna thinks about weekends at the Vega house. Henry spends Sundays cooking Paella with Lisa. When her father emerges from a steamy bathroom smelling like Edge shaving gel, did Lisa ignore him? more concerned with hanging out and the things of *Teen People*. If he insists upon paying attention to her, can she? At that age, it's all about who is paying the most attention. Anna remembers.

On Sunday mornings amid the waft of bacon and pancakes, Anna's father used to whistle the tune to *And I Think I'm Going Out of My Head*. He had this weird idea that it was all about ownership. He owned it. It would always be right where he'd left it when he'd turned his head. It. Anna.

Anna asks Henry if he carrys a picture of his daughter. He hesitats for a second but then reaches around for his wallet. He pulls out last year's school photo from behind an AMOCO credit card. She lets him just turn it to face her. She wonders if, knowing all too well what women are, it frightens him; here she comes sneaking up on him, the one he helped create. Will he run? By standing with Anna he's already gunning the engine that will carry him away. Our choices are what define us.

Anna steps back and lifts her drink. "Gorgeous hair," she remarks with a laugh. In a few years, Anna thought, that look in her eye will change ever so slightly.

"My very first love affair ended badly,"Anna says licking lime pulp off her lipstick."My father had a 1968 Cutlass F85. He used to let me sit on his lap and steer her out of the driveway. The sticky summer-hot black vinyl roll and tuck and all the things that over time had gotten lost in it shaped me. I thought my father knew how much I loved that car, 'cause when I asked, he promised to keep it for when I was old enough to drive it. Can you see me in that car?

"Anyway, I thought he realized how, since I said something about it, I must have meant it. But one day my father left it at the park and ride in the morning like he always did, and for $250.00 some stranger got to drive it away."

"Oh, come on," Henry scoffed. "I'd do the same thing."

"Listen Henry," Anna said. "I'm in my thirties, and am hanging out in a no-name bar on a work night telling a married man this story. A little something you might want to think about before you do the same thing."

Henry pointed to Anna's empty. "How many have you had?"

The front line.

Intellectually, Anna knew that this was Henry's game now. She understood that. And when she'd first claimed this position— legs crossed against the cold, suede gloved hands tucked up underneath her arms and the shoulder straps of her purse, a shopping bag from Saks holding an expensive bottle of wine poorly—she found some humor in her waiting covertly at the intersection of something and Main at the height of Friday evening rush hour. But then Anna heard these two people shouting outside the Cucina with the sad potted evergreens flanking the door. The accusations rose and fell in the wind. "I wasted thirty-two years of my life on you. You're doin' to me exactly what my papa did to my Momma. How could I have been so stupid!"

Ain't it always that way? Anna thought.

Like a dog who smells a cancer, Anna tried to move herself away, out of range. But not so far that she couldn't keep checking up and down the street for Henry, and occasionally on the shouting. Three people. Two women and a man. Two dressed for dinner. One wrapped tight in an out-of-date coat with three quarter sleeves—a car coat, it used to be called. Anna felt an hysterical kind of laughter tickling the back of her throat. She needed to pee. The cold sometimes did that to her.

"Listen," Henry said when Anna got into his car with the tinted glass. "I wasn't yelling at you yesterday."

"Yes. You were," Anna said, slipping into the empty brown ball cap that was thrown on the dash. It was soft and warm and shaped like him.

"I wasn't. You were just acting crazy, shouting across the street like that, at five o'clock in the afternoon, next to the park. My daughter could have been hanging there. After we do this, you can't stop me in the street any more. You can't come looking for me."

Anna was electrified by this man explaining the obvious in a way which would imply that English might not be her thing. "Boy, this seat is really far forward," Anna said.

"So move it back."

Henry jumped on the expressway, got off in Woodhaven near the BQE. Anna turned to him, "Come on Henry, tell me a nice lie."

"Momma, what are you talking about?"

"Tell me something nice."

"Why would it be a lie?"

"It would. But I still want to hear it."

"I'm not going to lie to you."

Anna knew he meant for the moment, not not ever.

After an animated reenactment of what seemed a volatile encounter with his supervisor and his union rep earlier in the week, Henry put his foot on the edge of the motel bed and started untying his Air Jordan.

"Go on,"Anna urged.

"I wasn't sure."

"Right."

"You scare me, Momma. Worse than the front line."

Three-day Expedite

Anna disobeys a direct order and pushed off the bus long before her stop to check to see if the truck parked beside the middle school was his. She walked neither swiftly nor slowly, just walked. To see. She slipped between the truck and a parked car to better see the arched handle of a hand truck in a shaded courtyard. There was a back to her, but she decided the hair was not enough gray and Anna was disappointed even before some other driver tossed her a curious glance.

Anna was wearing new shoes and was miserable in the thought of trudging the rest of the way home, even though it was still light and she might legitimately yet come across Henry making pick-ups. Pick-ups were last in the day; favorite customers very last, as a courtesy. Anna struggled home. Someone was going to have to break her legs to get her to stop.

Anna unlocked her front door, ignored the mail and went straight for a corkscrew. She twisted and yanked thinking about the motel. About his story. The foot soldier, breaking bones jumping out of airplanes in the middle of the night at eighteen ("Don't let anyone tell you they don't shit their pants the first time!"); sniping Iraqi generals in their red BMWs on their way home to their families at thirty ("I've still got one guy's wallet."); Package Car Driver, still.

Anna'd somewhere heard the company described as heavily fortified. It seemed apt. From what Henry told, it fostered an entirely Us-against-Them mentality. Every day began with security cameras and roll calls, locker rooms and degradation. Uniforms that didn't always fit but had better be finished off with spit-shined shoes. The man found comfort in the structure; a civilian who still clipped his hair short and did rounds and rounds of push, pull and sit ups. But at thirty-nine he was feeling a little too old to be told every day he was a fuck up. So he tweaked the system any way he could and liked to sue people. He sued a customer a few blocks away from Anna whose slate step had been loose and who had laughed when he slipped and fell. ("If she didn't laugh, I wouldn't have taken her for that 7K.") He sued Pontiac because after keeping his car for a month, they still couldn't figure out why the check engine light wouldn't go off. He had had to take off work to make trips to Small Claims Court and won a settlement of three-thousand dollars—two thousand less than he was out-of-pocket, all totaled, but he *won* the judgment, and that was all that mattered.

Anna stood at her kitchen counter wrestling with a cork, making lists of excuses for his bad behavior. He's in Florida was his daughter, it's Spring Break. No, she thought. I pass Lisa's school on my way out every morning. The yard's still full of little posses. Oh, it's Passover. He's hanging around while his wife's family lights candles. No. Not likely. OK. He's bleeding in Afghanistan. Well, I hope to death!

Henry shouldn't have told Anna that, yeah, he's lucky he lives in his own route.

"Yeah, it's cool," he tells Anna with lifted brows like it's an inside joke. "I can keep an eye on Lisa after school; except she hits me up for money every time she sees me."

His wife has no face. It's Lisa Anna wants to replace.

Office Affair

There is a pink Post-It note sticking to my computer monitor that says "Good Dog" in clear, bold, Sharpie marker. One day my boss, the publisher at a house that still regarded itself boutique in spite of the entertainment conglomerate's logo on all of our ID cards, asked me if it was my network password. I could imagine that she had never once seen it hanging off my forehead after I'd had to fetch her from the lobby, too drunk from lunch to make it back up to the twenty-fourth floor on her own, or upon having spent an entire morning five days before Christmas with her corporate AMEX and an American Girl catalog deciphering her nine-year-old daughter's scrawl.

I spend a lot of my time picking up after her. Book proposals would sometimes be stuck together by the Nicorette she'd pull from her mouth during marketing meetings. Coffee stirrers would be strewn like pick-up sticks in the layer nearest to the cherry veneer of her ergonomic specific, custom-made desk—two for every empty mug strewn around the room. I'd think I'd found them all, and then later in the day, I'd follow my nose to a mug propping up some jacket art on the credenza, something beyond description settled at the bottom.

Some clever designer in the art department presented me with a mug of my own embossed with a yellow traffic sign that read Bitch At Work. Original. I left it beside the pantry sink where it could play with the ones from NPR and Book of the Month Club. I felt strongly that having an office mug, a personalized screen saver, shoes in a bottom drawer, would marry me to this job. Unless you counted the Post-It and a wallet-size NASCAR Winston Cup schedule I'd picked up at the newsstand in the lobby, my cubicle said nothing of me.

Around 9:25, the strange little bird who works for the executive editor and occupies what was once the vacant desk in the next stable over from me, arrives cupping the last of a corn muffin to her chest. About a month after Lucy started, I discovered that she took her meals in the last stall of the ladies' room off the reception area; I had recognized her skinny ankles seemingly in repose. "I don't like having my breakfast in the middle of the hallway," Lucy explained standing at the sink washing the evidence of a greasy egg sandwich away.

In the morning before turning on her computer, Lucy unfurls a plum Loreal lipstick that she dabs across her lower lip while pouting into the shiny end of the tube. Lucy is a size two soaking wet, with huge breasts. Every time she got out of her chair, I'd look, hoping to catch the moment gravity toppled her over. Otherwise, I didn't dislike her.

Lucy is being chased across the aisle between us by her swivel chair. Her computer is groaning into life behind her.

"There's this boy," she says conspiratorially. "He's in a band. And they are playing at the Bank in a couple of weeks, you know on Valentine's Day. I want to take him home with me. I know he knows I like him and he's playing hard to get."

"And?" I say. Beyond commiserating about weird phone calls, Lucy and I usually did not confide.

"And, I sit next to you for God-sakes. I've been watching."

"You've been what?"

"Just tell me what you'd do."

I tossed a Starbucks cup into my empty wastebasket, the first trash of the day, and licked some sugary foam off my thumb. "You want my advice? Just look him in the eye and tell him what you want. Boys are lazy, and love, love, love when the girl does all the work."

Lucy looks satisfied, as most people are when what they hear supports what they already want to believe. "Thanks," she says, kicking her way, seat and all, back to her own desk. "You always seem to know how to get exactly what you want."

"Is that what it looks like from over there?"

The exchange with Lucy perplexed me, and over-caffeinated, I stood beside one of three Rubermaid garbage tubs filing. I am almost done with the explosion that is the out box my boss leaves for me like cookies for Santa every night; papers, books, ribbed plastic salad containers from the cafeteria, sometimes slip out of the wire basket, and if I was lucky, onto a guest chair, but most times to the floor. Pencils in the out box simply mean she wants them replaced with taller, sharper ones.

I'm almost done when I hear the jungle rhythm of the publisher's bangles working the hall. I gather as much as I can in my arms and gaze longingly at the view—the rooftop garden outside the private dining rooms on the twelfth floor, the neon marquee of Radio City Music Hall, the majesty of the CBS Building known as Black Rock an arm's reach away—before I sequester myself in the hall with buzzing flourescent tubes, Formica and acoustic tile.

In addition to trafficking wine-stained confidential inter-office correspondence, as Publisher's Assistant I was often putting great prizes into other people's hands. I went out of my way to acquire through the purchasing department and thus at great discount an Aeron chair for an author with a weak spine. I put the memoirist, who had provided me the great opportunity to hold a check for three million dollars before over-nighting it to her Panama City address, in Ted Turner's private sky box for the last game of the playoffs. While I, heaved a carton of expensive art books for Ted's assistant down to Fed-Ex after hours with a smile. A novelist on a frantic book tour would call me and not her publicists to get her out of coach and into first class. This same woman phoned me from a Barnes and Noble in Berkeley to ask me if I happened to know anyone in town who could teach her how to surf. As it turned out, I did. She reached me the next morning, her voice thick with a pleasure I'd rather not define, to thank me; to ask me how I came to know such interesting people.

Today my boss is wearing a cape. At least that's what it looks like. I follow at her heels and catch what I can while she talks to her monitor, checking the e-mail that has accumulated in the night. Mostly though, I am staring at Black Rock.

I usher my boss into an editorial meeting with her gum, Uniballs and three New York City dailies open to the gossip pages. The office is quiet when I call CBS Sports. I speak to someone who is nice, and like me, works for the person in charge. Turns out she's been wanting a copy of the seventy-five dollar coffee table book by the celebrity wedding planner that is expected out later in the spring; I have binder's copies hidden under my desk. I reach between my legs to pet one as I negotiate. She's getting married in the fall and wants this book bad. She offers up a prize beyond my imagining; an invitation to drop in on day two of the Daytona Pre-production meeting when "the boys," as she puts it, break for lunch; she can because she's the one who's planned it.

"Who is it you said you wanted to meet?"

"Ned Jarrett," I confirm. Letting the name of the Winston Cup champion, retired the year I was born, rush off my tongue.

I'd started watching NASCAR young—a mystery to my urbane parents was how such a thing began when I wasn't generally allowed TV at all. My livingroom fandom predated restricter plates and cable TV, back when the drivers all sported a similar backwoods fashion in facial hair and with slow-and-easy drawls particular to a family clan as well as a geographic region. Early on, I decided I am an Allison and not a Petty. A Jarrett and not an Earnhardt. It was the curiously soothing sounds of their voices long before their skill behind the wheel or the brightly colored sponsor products—most of which I was too young to legally use—that elicited my loyalty.

I'd been to the South. That is to say that I had been as far as Miami on I-95. How do you spell that? my mother would snap when, over roasted chicken at our dinner table, I'd slip into my version of the lazy vernacular of a modern-day Scarlett. Neither do I sound like I am from New York City. Raised by an English major, there is no Long Island drawl or Queens nasal, or any corner in Brooklyn in my voice. Diction, vocabulary, awareness of one's own tongue, these I had.

I was a consistent, though not fanatical, viewer through the years; lately I'd been catching the ESPN Classics series of disconcertingly sepia-toned races from the eighties that aired just after prime-time. Like a colicky baby, I was tranquilized by Ned's sure race commentary. I spent Sunday afternoons from February to November on the couch at the very edge of REM sleep, jerked in and out, not by commercial interruptions, but by a disconnect in the constant vvrroom by a shuffling of cars on a tri-oval, or the pulses of Ned's observations. But, I've never been to a race. The idea of 150,000 people in one place—well, actually, the epic wait to get back out of the parking lot which might very well last longer than the race itself, upsets my sensibilities. Besides, TV offered me Ned.

I dress carefully the next day. I put on my best Bendel's suit, and pearls because they seem gentile and Southern to me. And whatever affect I have created, I either punctuate or erase with the reddest lipstick I own. I almost get hit by a car when I jay-walk across the Avenue at exactly 11:53. I'm stopped at security in the lobby of the CBS building; I can barely utter my name. I'm stopped again at reception on my counterpart's floor and am told to sit but don't. I keep searching through the tinted glass behind the operator's head. Three people pass behind without noticing me.

My fairy-godmother is shorter than she sounds. I tower over her in my heels when we shake hands. I hand her the size eleven Jiffy bag with the goods.

"Oh, let's drop this off at my desk before we go up," she says. We begin to wind through a typical office labyrinth so familiar that I seem to know where to go before I'm told. "I asked Ned if this was all right," she says. I try hard to swallow; it takes two or three neck contortions.

"I told him that you thought he was the epitome of the southern gentleman." The walk was making her winded. "And you know what he said?"

"What's that?" I was beginning to dislike her.

"'Fooled another one.' Isn't that funny? I've met his wife. She's a wonderful woman. They're perfectly suited."

Without warning she pushes herself against a double door and we are inside a media room. A large knot of men are huddled beside a buffet, including Ned's oldest son who, down on pit-road, wears his CBS blue, but I see the racing legend immediately in a group of three beside the windows, his plume of silver hair disbursing the sun. I disconnect from my guide and make my way across the room through a thrum of testosterone that is not entirely displeasing.

Ned is expecting me. Their conversation drops away and this Yankee extends her hand. "This is an honor," I say, perfectly.

I have no idea what time it is when I get back and head straight for the ladies' room, which is vacant except for a toothbrush someone has left on the back of one sink. I slide into a stall and into the space between the bowl and the partition, gathering my long wool coat over one arm so that it won't drape on the floor. I ignore the fact that someone's come through the door and that only one of my feet will be seen if they look. There's a slam-click and the collective partitions shudder against my shoulder. I do not stop what I am doing. In fact, I find an even better angle. I hear the rustle of a candy wrapper.

"You're back late," Lucy says. "There's a three-hundred page manuscript on your desk that your boss wants a copy of to take home. I think it's two sided."

The Scientologist with
Situational Ethics

Anna filled the bar stool next to Mark and produced her Amex in one fluid movement like an actress in a defining role. Anna was used to paying his way. No sooner had she crossed her legs than he started to jiggle the ice in his spiked club soda.

"What's that?" Anna pointed to his glass. She wanted to be sure he was drinking drinking. Mark had just come from some chic salon and cocked his colorful high-and-low-lights like a bird. Nearly a decade ago, Anna had worked at a record company and Mark had been receiving platinum album awards, and they had had the same long hair as everyone else—just better. Anna couldn't help but miss his, visibly, even rudely. Enough for Mark to squeeze some of Anna's thigh and hiss "fleshy" with a corresponding irrelevant mourning.

And yet, Mark and Anna systematically sought each other's company when feeling anxious or desperate for a renewed sense of self. Though lately it had begun to feel more like reliving a plot in a movie whose ending is predictable and boring. Mark crunched vodka soaked ice between worn complaints and sour disillusionments, describing to her once more the uneasy state of everyday failing at his marriage.

He and Anna sat facing each other, though eyes looking past. Mark tapped another Nat Sherman against the pack. "I've got to be home by ten."

"Of course," she said. She found Mark's attempt at self restraint endlessly amusing.

"No. Really. I can't leave the cats alone for so long."

"But they are cats."

"They're her cats," Mark said. "And they both have some kind of urinary infection. I've had my nose in their litter box for the last ten days. This is the first time I've been out all week."

Mark had called Anna Tuesday last, the morning after his wife had come home with an animal communicator. The group gathered in the living room amid the cluster of bordello-looking floor lamps that were trying hard to be a collection, and the usually disaffected felines began to shockingly behave like pets and circled with immediate interest, excited to have a translator. His wife busied herself taking notes and collecting food stuffs and toys from various rooms for a pass-or-fail grade.

"They seemed very clear," Mark said. "On what they wanted to eat, what was helping them and what they would rather do without."

I'd be thrilled too, Anna thought, at the opportunity.

"She told us, the animal communicator, that Willow, the bigger cat, is my creative partner and he's the one who helps me catch the music."

"So what you are saying," Anna said. "Is that I'm off the liner notes entirely now."

Over a stainless steel basin, Anna shook the water off her hands and assessed herself in the bathroom mirror with a practiced distraction. There it was, the deliberate smear of good cosmetics and that achingly familiar look one gives oneself after thirty. Because of these disconcerting, mildly-educational aspects to Anna's body, it made her careful to only consider sleeping with a peer.

Anna unapologetically brushed against Mark's unmoving knees to sit back down and reported, "By the way, the bathroom stall has a full door that locks with a deadbolt." But Anna's suggestion was intercepted by a waitress in a slinky dress who'd rather superfluously since they were seated at the bar, slid her tray beneath her breasts and in front of Mark's chin, to ask if she could entice him with an Appletini, perhaps. Desert, maybe?

Mark's head bobbed from her to Anna who sat back to better frame the shot. Through a plume of blue cigarette smoke Anna said "You can dial it back. Your tip relies on my generosity, not his."

Mark laughed when the waitress went away. "Proprietary, not jealous—I remember." It was his little self-satisfied laugh which made his lip curl like a surprised window shade.

"She's cutting in on my time," Anna said loudly when the waitress returned to relieve her tray of their drinks.

"So," Mark said. "Did you bring a check?"

Anna had promised to loan him the money to join the Church of Scientology. "Yes," Anna said. "I want it back in one lump payment. No dollar here, dollar there thing."

"I know."

After a moment, Mark asked the ceiling, "What do you think would have happened if you and I had gotten married? You think we would have made it?"

"Check please."

In the street, Anna stopped the first yellow thing she saw. When sliding into the open mouth of the midtown tunnel, Anna was aware Mark was talking but she had too many other ideas to index. When they stopped on his corner she realized, if she'd chosen to acknowledge an almost imperceptible hesitation, she could have followed him upstairs. But she didn't. And her decision only concerned her in that this inaction might weaken the link—diminish the current. Regardless, some fish will always swim upstream.

Anna had to circle the apartment building where Mark lived for twenty minutes waiting for a section of New York City curb to become available. Mark's neighborhood was a tangle of one-way, one-lane streets and Anna blocked traffic while an Accord twisted and bounced out of a spot the driver was regretful to lose.

She found Mark with the phone still in his hand, sitting at the kitchen table staring at some crooked nails in the blank canvas of a wall. His wife had taken all the good stuff and what was left was scattered everywhere, some of it broken. At three in the morning, and at the bottom of a questionable bottle of B & B she'd found under the sink, Anna had finished classifying stage clothes by tour, making separate pile for this year's and last season's surf attire. Mark sang her Alanis Morrisette songs from a square of floor that the day before had been beneath an heirloom Persian rug. His renditions were astonishingly more self-pitying than the originals. After considering all night the rebar hung vertically on the walls at eighteen inch intervals, Anna finally asked, "What the hell are those for?" And he said reasonably, "Radionics."

"I guess it didn't work," Anna said.

After another night of sorting through the sticky shit at the back of some other woman's kitchen drawers, Anna helped move all of what remained into her basement and one of the hall closets. Temporary storage, Mark kept telling her. He wandered around her home saying that Yes, he remember This, that That looked familiar. Anna stopped at a mini-mart for cigarettes and some half and half, both for her, before taking Mark back to his

empty apartment. Mark pressed himself against the passenger
door. He took her hand off the gear shift. "Can't I just move into
your place?"

The way Mark scoured the aisles at Fresh Fields was amusing
at first. The way he contemplated his way through produce,
pondered potions and powders around fresh gluten-free bread
endcaps, viscus liquids in eye dropper bottles, oh the many and
varied brands of liquid soy, fruit juices and raw sugar. He lost
her in the cereal section and found her at the seafood counter.

"The tuna looks good," he tells her. He raises his voice. "Is
that sushi grade?"

"Of course," the fishmonger tells him, his plastic gloved fingers poised over the stack of oval steaks, ringed like slices of a
tree trunk.

"Two please."

"And a half a pound of sea scallops," Anna says.

At the point of purchase, Mark adds two citronella candles to
the cart.

"What are those for?"

"There must have been a half a dozen mosquitos in your
house last night. The last thing I need is West Nile."

"Geriatrics and children, Mark. Not healthy men in their
thirties, juiced up on two hundred dollars worth of organic
food."

"I'm not taking any chances."

The cashier interrupts. "That will be one hundred eighty six
dollars and fifteen cents."

"I was close," Anna says.

"How about I pay next time."

Anna hands over her debit card. "Help bag."

At Five Boro, drinks were served in mason jars accompanied
by rubber geckos with suction cups for feet. There was always a

large colony sticking to the bar where the music was loud, voices louder still and surfaces gritty with citrus and salt.

Anna imagined herself in Mexico, perhaps sun-stroked and free spirited, letting her thigh slide between the end pieces of a sarong. She conjured a tan she did not have, exhibitions of speech and gesture. She loudly made fun of some other women there. It was like riding a bike, this habit that she had given up and could not remember why. The guy next to Anna was describing how he used the top of his Alopecia-smooth head when performing cunnilingus.

Anna was sure it was because of some chemical leeching from the geckos—particularly the pink ones—that made Mark's mouth find hers. They groped for a while more excited by the public nature of the situation. By the shock of it. By the melted cheese and refried beans of it. Anna wrapped her legs around his and found his frail response less of an invitation than she might need to continue.

Have another gecko," she told him handing him a full jar.

"What's the matter?"

"I'm looking for bulk."

The next morning Anna poured Rice Dream in her coffee by mistake. It curdled on contact.

"It's what you should be drinking anyway," Mark said from the table. "Aren't you lactose intolerant?"

"No, hung over. You need to find a place to live."

"There's a moody looking boy out front asking for you." The receptionist peered over the half-wall of Anna's cubicle. The pink of his Oxford almost exactly matched the sheen of his skull.

"A what? Who?"

"He said his name is Mark. I forget, is he the one I'm not supposed to let back here?"

"Well, who is out there stopping him now if he were?"

The receptionist turned on his heel and waved his empty coffee mug at her. "I'm on my break."

Anna's thighs pressed against the beveled edge of her desk. She leaned over and checked both ways down the hall like she was crossing the street and then fell again into the tulip cup of her executive assistant chair; it differed from an editorial assistant chair in that it did not lack arms.

"Who's here?" Lucy asked, slapping a sheaf of pages on her desk before grabbing its edge to roll her armless chair back underneath. Office aerobics. Lucy's face was flushed from having been digging under her desk through the piles of unread manuscripts she kept hidden from view.

"Mark," Anna said.

"Oh." Lucy blew out the corner of her mouth to dislodge a shock of red hair. "And?"

"And, I've no idea. I can't imagine. Should I leave him out there?"

Lucy clown-grinned at Anna. "Do I have lipstick on my teeth?" She had the cap in one hand and the hyper-extended smoosh of colored wax in the other. Anna couldn't look away from the ski-jump shape of Lucy's plum colored wax.

"No. But, why do you care?"

"Why not? It's pretty boring around here, haven't you noticed?"

"I had."

"Besides, if I remember correctly, doesn't Mark look a little like David Foster Wallace? You know how I feel about DFW."

"What? No. Well, maybe a little. No." Anna looked again down the hall, which was empty. "How do you get lost from reception to here?"

Mark arrived with a new camera rig around his neck. Extra lenses and other accouterments filled a pink and white 47th Street Photo shopping bag.

"What's all that?" Anna said.

"I thought I'd give it a whirl. I've been wanting to."

"That's the best idea you've had yet," Anna said.

"I thought we were getting along," Mark said leaning an arm on Lucy's partition.

"I've got an old Cannon," Lucy said. "I took some great shots of shadows in Barcelona last summer."

"My father's a photographer. He won awards for some stop-action photos of a Mexican road race in '53. One of the first motor-drive sequences on record. They're on permanent exhibit in Japan."

"Mark's never taken a picture in his life," Anna said.

"Some Polaroids."

"Yeah, of who?" Anna said.

"A."

"Who's A?" Lucy asked, reaching behind her to pull on the strap of her minimizer.

"The one who got away," Anna said.

"Racing," Lucy processed. "You're into those motor-sports, aren't you Anna?"

Mark said, "I think she watches Bull Riding these days. Likes to see guys get kicked in the head."

"So what's up, Mark?" Anna said. "This is where I work, remember?"

"You're off soon, right? I thought we could go home together,"

"Funny. That doesn't have the ring to it once might have had."

Mona

In Ranch Country
Men are Valued by their
Ability with Horses

I'm not too sure what made me agree to have a drink in town with Chad, exactly. Company most likely. I'd summarily rejected any prospect of companionship at the Owl Hoot Artists Residency where I was a third through my stay, though the residency director insisted that part of the criteria for acceptance is the individuals probability of providing a well-rounded artistic experience to the rest of the mix. I was not an unpleasant guest. I was willing, though not anxious to make friends. Dinners ended early. No one lingered. It was still day when I went into my room to change my clothes for drinks.

Curiosity had made me go back to the ranch for another trail ride and ostensibly my first lesson from Chad on what a real cowboy is as opposed to a fake. That afternoon, Chad had taken me out behind the ranch buildings, again through the swift moving Piney Creek and up the jagged edge of a bluff to show me some Crow tee-pee rings hidden in the brome. In the end, I'd agreed to the drink, I think, because I didn't want to disappoint the ranch owner Jeb who was standing beside the corral when Chad and I came off the prairie soaked to the bone.

The sky held no grudge against the mid-afternoon storm and streaks of bright sunlight crossed the quilt on my bed. Eventide, I thought. An archaic word, however appropriate here.

He'd put me back on Sparky who was slightly more resigned though still none too happy about the weight of my ass on his back, especially when someone let the herd out to pasture and my horse saw his friends flashing colors through the cotton woods. Sparky tossed his head high, and impossibly tried to turn around. His shoes clacked on loose rock and occasionally his knees buckled.

Chad kicked his horse up to the top of the bluff. "We're here." Chad was seated in his saddle right; knees perfectly straight. The reins were slack in his hand, and he guided his horse with a subtle shifting of his thighs. His horse stepped delicately, tracing the two hundred year old tee-pee and fire rings just about invisible in the grass to someone level with the ground. Chad pointed his hat down left and then right over each shoulder, and told me the story of the lichen covered rocks as he no doubt had heard it being told. I only heard some things. I was too busy feeling the dance that Sparky had decided to do. "Makes sense," Chad went on. "We're about five hundred feet above the valley. You can see the whole plain from here. There's Owl Hoot, over there. Young Crow, on the lookout for hostile New Yorkers," he said.

Sparky cut his circles tighter. I felt his increasing agitation. Chad stopped his horse suddenly and looked at the sky. Sparky refused to stand still, but there was a lot more room up on the bluff and so I didn't care. "What?" I asked, the tableau spinning. That's when the hail began.

I was laughing at first. Sparky did not agree with the humor and then I was horizontal like a bronc rider. Sparky came down hard and I slid against the saddle horn. There was half a breath before Sparky took off, running like he meant it with another square state on his mind. I smelled leather and what was the straining engine of my determined horse. Ice hammered my head and stung where there was bare skin. My hands were slick but when I had the courage to look the reins were still there. My hair was wet and heavy and slapped me in the back while Sparky was kicking up the earth, trying to run away from the weather. I had no idea how far we were from Chad and what might happen when we ran out of flat. Chad was nowhere. I had no technique but neither was I hanging off the saddle. I pulled on Sparky's reins but he didn't seem to mind the poor aerodynamics of racing with his head in the air.

Chad came up on us, riding with just his legs and grabbed at what he expected to be runaway reins. For a while the animals were in perfect sync and it was beautiful. At once, Chad's horse broke away and the wrangler had Sparky by the throat. I waited for Chad to tell me what to do. The dark of my horse's eyes had disappeared, but he slowed enough for Chad's feet to get hold of the dirt.

In the storm, Chad shouted for me to step off. "Get down," he said with a seriousness that made me hurry. "We're going to do this the cowboy way. Chad held Sparky's bridle while the animal heaved between us. "Hold on to him while I go and get mine.

I wondered what made Chad choose Sparky out of all the other horses in the barn as my match. The hail was evenly mixed with rain. Chad walked his horse around so that he and I could stand pressed between the two animals to wait out the storm. He closed the open end of the triangle with his back. I could smell the minerals rising in the steam off the ground, the simmering panic in the skittish horses and the loam of Chad's drooping hat.

"Lesson one," Chad said. "This is why most don't like cow-boying in the winter." Ice clattered in the brim of his hat. There was that and the noise of breathing.

"This is winter?"

"Just about."

I liked it here because unlike in the Big Stinky, people take their cues from instinct, weather, large things, not trends or Simon Says. No one asks too many questions here. No one really cares where you came from, or which direction you're headed when you leave. Just about the job you do, that you do it well, and respect the men who've taught you how. For this reason, I like it here very much—the honesty of hard work and all that. Blue collar attraction, firemen, cops, steel-workers…cowboys. Chad's accused me of being on the run, in between. I don't mind so much this qualifier; it's what he can see and there's no way he can know the rest.

"And are you most?" I said.

"Haven't decided. Probably."

I called out to Jeb as Chad and I took a short cut through the parking area toward the barn, "I'm thinking this is a good look for me." Conversation kept my teeth from chattering.

"Aw, you're pretty any which way," Jeb said. "My wrangler here would own you a shot or two if he were old enough to buy 'em." The old man slapped Chad on the ass the way he did his favorite head of stock. Laughing out the side of his mouth, Jeb walked away, missing every mud filled puddle, not giving much thought to the facility provided by his bowleggedness.

Without being told, I brought Sparky to the barn door. "How old are you?"

"Twenty this past July." Chad nodded at my horse. "You can give him to me." Chad took the reins out of my hand. "Oh, come on," Chad said. "What does it matter?" I watched him disappear into the shadows; I waited for something else, but heard only the clacking of the horses' feet on dirt so dry and compact it's like concrete.

It is a Browning .30–.06 in the rack, Chad told me when I asked. He pulled against the curb, close, two tires in the gutter. I told him I knew the landmark neon of the Stove-Up Saloon from before I ever thought twice about the square state. I had to laugh a little that I was back in the Stove-Up two nights in a row, walking around with someone named Chad, who holds open the door.

We settled in at the end of the bar. Across from the juke box. I hooked my heels over the brass and leaned over the lip of a bar that's been smoothed by the underside of generations of fore-arms. The bartender nodded at me and then raised an eyebrow at Chad who had his head down. She was deep in conversation with a narrow man in a J.B. Hunt baseball cap. I hadn't noticed the string of amber lights that outlined a Peterbilt across the street. She leaned in, flicked her long dark hair over her shoulder, rapt until the man finished his yarn, even while he took long drags off a Camel where all the commas are.

Chad played with his dingy belt buckle.

"How'd you get that anyway?" I asked.

Chad scooted back, away from where I'd reached. "The usual way. I won it."

"Doing what?"

"Shoveling horse-shit."

"Be that way," I said looking again down the length of the bar. "I'm parched, aren't you?"

"Riding bulls," Chad answered finally. "Made a mess of my bladder. You'll see, I have to piss every—"

"Eight seconds?" I laughed.

"You're funny, Mona."

The bartender came over wiping her hands on a rag. "I'm Janis. What can I get you tonight?" She had a look like she'd set up a joke and was ready to be amused. From under his misshapen hat, Chad said, "Bud Light."

"I'll have a double Beam and Coke, short."

Janis reached for a glass. Filled it with ice and said, "Hey cowboy, I'll need to see some ID."

Chad patted himself all the places where his wallet might have been. A bottle of Beam hovered longingly over my glass and Janis held her other hand on her hip.

"I must have left my wallet in my work truck," Chad said.

Janis looked out the window. "And what would you call that thing you've got outside?"

"Would you like to see mine?" I said, hoping to draw attention away.

"Sure," Janis said. "New Yawk City!" Janis announced. A couple of people near the front window acknowledged the occasion. It took Janis a moment to find my birth date. "Lord girl," Janis whooped. "You're older than I am."

I held out a hand for either my license or my drink, I didn't care which. Janis, genuinely curious, turned the card over to examine the other side before she handed it back.

"Thanks," I said. Janis slid me my drink, reached into a cooler and yanked back the top of Chad's beer. She was still holding it when she said laughing, "So tell me. How does a kid like you find a gal from New York Citeee?"

With a little bit of knowing in his voice, Chad said, "I work at a guest ranch."

"Well here cowboy." Janis passed him the can and before walking away said, "I wouldn't want to be the one to deny either of you the experience."

"I don't know how I feel about that remark," I said.

"I'm all right with it." Chad said tipping his head back. The beer did not wash away the bit of chew caught near his gum line.

"No wallet. I guess to keep up the charade I'll have to pay your tab," I said.

"I'll buy you breakfast someday."

I got up and loaded the jukebox with Marshall Tucker and Chris LeDoux. "You know, I've been thinking," I said leaning on the lighted glass. I'm pretty sure I lost my virginity the year you were born."

Chad sat perfectly still. "So did my mother. You know," Chad said. "I've been thinkin', you should get yourself a pair of Rockies. You've got the best kind of ass for jeans with no hip pockets."

"Haven't any of your friends warned you that someday someone might make you put your money where your mouth is?"

"I've got a leg up on my friends. It's just been my mother, my sister and me. I've spent my whole life around the habits of two crazy women. I know when to duck."

"The real secret, Chad. Is to not be so cocky about it."

Wick broke through the murk back by the pool table. "Yeah, Chad," Wick drawled. "Better do what the lady tells ya." Wick positioned himself between Chad and me to drain the last of a Coors. His forearms were a canvas of hand-poked tattoos depicting poorly rendered skulls and rattle snakes. The barbed wire that wrapped from shoulder to wrist had been beaten to a sea-slime green by his proximity to the sun. Wick put his beer down. "See ya later Miss Janis."

"See ya around, Wick," Janis answered also checking the level of my drink. "Friend of yours," Janis asked Chad.

"Same ranch," Chad said.

"Small town," I said. In a minute I asked, "Hey Chad, I have a question. I hear in ranch country the men are valued most for their ability with horses. Who were you saving this afternoon?"

"Well, it wouldn't be right coming back with just one of you. It would take a mighty long time to pay the ranch back for a lame horse on six dollars an hour."

Mona's String

The Stove-Up Saloon is full of the guest ranch girls who are playing cowboy for the summer and draw the wranglers into town from four directions every Saturday night. From behind the bar Janis took their photo ID and their daddy's credit cards in turn, and knew their names by the second week of June.

Mona's staying another winter which makes her a local. Since befriending Janis, Mona'd come to know all the characters with the authority of a lifer, though it's occurred to her in parts that she'll never blend.

One night Janis slides Mona a torn square of 120 grit sandpaper. "This is for you."

"What's this?"

Janis lifts Mona's drink and wipes the bar with a rag that smells terrible. "Well Miss, it looks like a phone number to me. Poor boy came up to me and asked if I could please give this here to just about the prettiest gal he's ever seen in all of Wyoming," Janis incants for him.

"Sandpaper Janis. This is a true Wyoming moment."

"Yeah, well we're resourceful around here," Janis said while already off in the other direction.

"Better than a number written on a T-Lock shingle," Bud said.

"But not as good as forming and bending numbers out of baling or barbed wire," Jessy said.

It was Jessy's friend Bud and his messy blond pony tail Mona'd asked Janis about the first night it began to snow. Janis said she'd heard Bud preferred to play with Percherons and lived off somewhere more like nowhere than Owl Hoot. Mona admired people whose source of income was not right away known. Leaning back on her barstool, Mona gave Bud a quick up and down and breathed in the sweet smell of wood smoke; she was pretty convinced, if pressed, Bud knew a few extra uses for a lariat.

"I've heard," Janis said. "He's known best for his big fucking hand gun."

".454," Bud said in to his MGD.

"Is that what you think we're talking about?" Janis said.

"That's what I supposed too," Jessy said evenly. Jessy said everything evenly. Mona was stricken when he quietly told her that her favorite pair of suede Justins made her look like a European tourist. He'd tease Mona that her "usual" just ruined two good drinks, like she'd never heard it before.

Maybe it was something about the Boy Scout-like law-enforcement patches Jessy wore, or the name tag, and the way Mona'd seen him strip off his uniform shirt in the parking lot outside the bar and put on something civilian before coming in to let some steam off. Tell of Jessy's adoring family sealed his stand-up, solid kind-of-guy persona. They also factored into something unconsciously alluring; something that kept building upon itself every time Mona saw him.

Mona scratches at the soft spot of prickly heat left over from all day sweating at the Owl Hoot rodeo. For just a moment, she's paying more attention to her rash than to Jessy or who is standing within earshot. She eyes the small bulge beneath Jessy's upper lip. Half moons of sweat soak him under the arms of his white Wrangler shirt. Mona smirks into the last of a drink. Maybe she shouldn't have said what she did during the barrel races, but the warm whiskey and the smorgasbord of cowboy butt behind the chutes made her feel a little bawdy.

Mona deliberately fingers the bulky ring crowning the knuckle of her middle finger. The one she'd designed and fabricated in her cramped out-house-cum-studio around an elk's eye tooth Jessy shouldn't have given her. In the record heat the ring slides around with ease. She stacks four near empty glasses and pushes them to the edge of the table between her and Jessy after she sees Janis has gone to plastic. Jessy takes off his hat with one hand and with the other wipes away the sweat that's threatening precipitation. Before yesterday's rodeo, Mona hadn't seen Jessy since she'd let him off the hook. She had a history of that. Allowing. You'd never guess it to look. That was probably it.

"Things found in a Wyoming truck," Mona said, having to move aside a Owl Hoot phone directory, two pairs of sunglasses, and a quilted flannel shirt with a hole in the elbow in order to get out of the cold April scree. There were .30–.06 casings in the scoop of the passenger door arm rest and a mixed cassette of pop music belonging to Jessy's pre-teen daughter on the floor. And the fabric softener sheets tucked up in the sun visors, she told him, weren't helping with the wet Retriever smell.

"Thanks for this," she said. "It's been taking two turns of the key lately."

"It's just the air/fuel mix," Jessy said. "Surprised it's taken this long. It's got to be adjusted to the altitude which means you'll probably need to take your car to Billings. No one around here will know how to fiddle with that computer. Though there might be someone on Dick Arsdale's place that would know."

"Who?"

"Dick Arsdale. I saw you dancing with him one night at the Stove-Up."

"Ooh," Mona said. "The man with the falling down Wranglers? I love him. He's the reason I stayed."

Jessy looked confused but polite. Mona said, "Well you've got to have wondered what brought me here. I'm sure you assumed it was a man."

"Well, I might have considered that a safe assumption. Just not one who's been married for forty years and who wears his pants 'round the crack of his ass."

"Mighty fine dancer, however," Mona said. "I was at the Stove-Up where no one knew me and I saw him and his wife hit the floor. There was no one else in the bar, it was just them on the squeaking wood and it was like watching Cinderella and her prince, they looked so right together. How can you not love them; he ordered a Harvey Wallbanger for her. And Janis, you know, for all the beer she opens and Mr. Beam and Coca Cola she pours, she knew how to make it, bless her. I had to stay."

"So what if not a cowboy?"

"Interesting story actually. I was offered an opportunity— over a very good martini I might add—to come out here for National Public Radio. Some navel gazing piece: What If…you drop a quintessential New York City girl in the middle of oh, some wilderness area, with a bottle of water and a topo map."

Jessy's eyes got wide.

"Some girls get scouted by *Playboy*; NPR finds me."

"I'll have to ask you about how all that went some other time," Jessy said. "What I want to know now is, you stayed, so what's been left behind?"

"All of it." Mona stared. Jessy took a hand off the wheel and pulled his Stetson farther down on his head. "So while it seems a foolish question," Mona said. "Given this town has all of three traffic lights…"

"I happen to know there are four."

"Ok, four," Mona said smiling. "How well do you know Mr. Arsdale?"

"That's an interesting story actually," Jessy said. "Got a call in the middle of the night from a game warden who said one of Arsdale's hands had seen someone poaching off the road. He was being pretty insistent that I come. Neither one of us were in the best of moods as you can well imagine, and we get there and find the guy and he points us in one direction and then another where there is a deer, a mulie, probably hit by a truck a month before. The guy thinks all this is hilarious until I find some crystal meth on him."

"Idiot," Mona said for once giving thought to the minutia of Jessy's job.

"That Arsdale name is a mainstay in these parts. You keep good company Mona." Jessy asked, "Your turn's here, right?"

He'd already tapped his signal so Mona didn't bother to answer. Mona lurched in the seat and all that was in the diamond plate tool box in the bed of the truck rattled as they went over an unexpected heave in the road.

"You were wearing a lilac shirt. The top two buttons were undone." Jessy pulled against the curb in front of the little yellow house Mona had an offer in to buy since selling a few pieces of jewelry on consignment at the taxidermy down the block from the Stove-Up. "When you were dancing with Dick that night."

"I was?"

"Yes Ma'am, you were."

Jessy'd been standing behind her at the chutes yesterday watching the tin-can races. Mona let one cowgirl cut her corners and fire back to where she came, then another before she said, "I think I could do that. Rather, I've done that, just without the barrels." Jessy took a step away. It made Mona, through the whiskey, realize how close he'd been. "Oh," Mona laughed. "Did I say that out loud? I'm sorry." She put her hand on his sleeve only. "I shouldn't have said that." Their two hat brims collided.

"Quite all right," Jessy said. He stood still a moment and then looked over his shoulder. "You'll have to pardon me, Mona. I have to see a man about a horse. For my wife."

Mona's had some number of admirers since arriving. Though Sandpaper Hank, who came to town once a month for "provisions" and stopped in to the saloon hoping to see Mona, was by far the most creative. "I was sitting at home thinkin' what do I need in town so I can see Mona's pretty smile. Lettuce, I need some lettuce. So I started up my truck and here I am," he'd told her once.

Janis calls them Mona's fan-club, not without some disdain for both sexes, and that Mona was like a new horse for them all to break.

Watching the thick vein pump in men's temples while they talked to her made Mona feel like a science experiment at times. She'd watch as they'd try to sort out the differences between them and, after a while, the question became might it be worth the buck off?

Western men, for all the purported hardness from the life-long difficulties of a perpetual thirty-mile-an-hour breeze, were deep down pretty maternal, attuned to the wants and behaviors of those different shaped mammals who spoke another language. But it was their choice to show that side or not, and they rarely let you forget it.

At the Stove-Up, everyone was so sun-and-beer drunk no one much noticed the deputy take a seat with her. Mona had spent the morning with her boot heels hooked into the gate of an empty chute, and couldn't decide who she was interested in watching more, the small but firm bull riders in all states of prayer, meditation, rodeo yoga and undress, preparing for their eight second rides, or the stock contractor's daughter, a petite blonde with a clipboard and laminates directing traffic and laughing at off-color jokes with the same effortlessness; who even in PRCA standard dress, didn't seem to be wilting in the heat like everyone else.

The bull waiting to be rode in the chute beside Mona breathed on her leg and spilled drool into the dirt. He was so close with eyes so resigned, Mona had to make an effort to remember that it wasn't a petting zoo, that she had sneaked into her spot armed with her favorite adage it was easier to get forgiveness than permission.

She pulled the day sheet out of her hip pocket. Ned Price it said, was who was calmly climbing into the chute beside her. The inside band of Ned's custom hat was pulled below the brim and against the back of his neck with the idea the hat would stay in place no matter what. Ned wore a thick gold watch, and the cuffs of his shirt were folded over and over to just below the elbow. The palms of his leather gloves were black with layers of sticky rosen.

Mona peered into the chute while four other cowboys helped keep the bull in line so Ned could get a good enough seat. Ned made many adjustments, repeating some twice. The last one had his hand to his balls. Ned looked toward Mona and gave a small tip of the hat motion. A bit of what had been caked in the hoof of the bull rained into the brim of Mona's Euro-hat, as Jessy called it.

"Jessy, I don't know what you're worried about," Mona says leaning back in her chair. "I've had relationships based around P.O. Boxes and pre-paid phone cards and this is not one of them."

When Mona'd checked her email with her morning coffee there had been one from Jessy that made her chest tight. Her hands shook just a little. She felt lonely for the first time since she'd started thinking of Owl Hoot as her home.

"You said it's just about you, and I believe you." Mona smiles and nods at the bar-back as the empty glasses are cleared. "But I have to tell you Jessy, if you were any other man in any other place, the sudden, oh, how might you say it in these parts—jug-handle—wouldn't be as cute."

"I don't know what to do when you talk to me that way." Jessy has to raise his voice over Gary Allen on the jukebox.

Mona wants a dance. And another drink. "You're the first one in a long time who gets me Jessy," Mona says standing up. She slides her palms against the thighs of her starched jeans. "I'm the ally. Make no mistake."

A man with a faded pink kerchief, square-knotted around his throat, is telling Janis a story; who's busy working a pencil into her long black hair.

"So this guy says to me, 'What's the emergency' and I wasn't really paying attention, so I say 'Owl Hoot, Wyoming.' So the guy says again, 'What's the emergency?' and I say, 'Emergency? There's no dang emergency.'" The man with the kerchief makes a big deal of removing the foam from the long hairs of his moustache. "The guy tells me, 'You've dialed 911, sir' and I tell him 'I dialed 4-1-1. I want the number to the Stove-Up Saloon.' He goes, 'Well, you'd better hang up.' I say, 'I reckon so.'"

The cowboys have taken to wearing Hawaiian shirts outside the arena and Wrangler had at last figured out comfort with the TwentyX brand everyone was wearing. Ned Price had changed into clean clothes and was ordering at the crowded bar. He stepped a little bit sideways to make room for Mona and her empty glass.

Natasha

Commerce

Tubac, Az., 2000

They met because of a dying horse, the first one Natasha had ever seen. She'd been in Tubac six months or so, teaching the use of pivotal memory in memoir to a bunch of seniors with cramped handwriting on the weekends and running the register at a small gallery-slash-bookshop twenty five hours a week. So, one might immediately assume Natasha met Luke, the popular western photographer, at her day job, but it was the horse. A tired old paint who had collapsed and fallen under some fence rails for which Luke had stopped his Escalade in the middle of the road.

Natasha came up on the scene, driving too fast and with the radio too loud not to be noticed by the clutch of men who were pulling unsuccessfully at a tow rope attached to the very old horse; so Natasha cut the engine and lit a cigarette.

The men were sweat-and-dirt soaked. Natasha had no idea a horse—even one lashing around with all four feet succeeding only in getting more tangled—could make such a noise. Only when the vet arrived did Luke make like he was going to move his truck. But first, he leaned against the door of Natasha's car, and with filthy fingers pinched fresh chew from a tin.

"He's going to shoot her," he said. Even Natasha could see the horse, though now free, was in bad shape. "The thing is," Luke said. "Horses are designed to stand and she was down too long. And what do you do with a dead horse? You leave them where they fall and wait for the dog food guy to come and get them." And this is how Natasha met Luke.

Sure she knew who he was, and that he was married. And in spite of the horse rescue or maybe because of the outcome, he turned to Natasha and said "I want to invite you to do something reckless." Natasha liked the way he put it. Sometimes, it's just that simple. Later that night after Natasha figured just getting on her back would be enough, Luke surprised her by taking an ankle in each hand, dragging her to the end of her small mattress to make himself more comfortable between her legs. Still, she sighed impatiently expecting the sort of eagerness when ambition gets ahead of intuition.

There was usually a balance to Natasha's relations: A lover's ego and Natasha's natural diffidence. For it was through men that Natasha got to know herself better, how she explored who she was. Different parts of herself in the form of different men. And yet as that first night with Luke progressed the way it did, she wanted to give in and this alarmed her. Slightly. It was as though she made some decision in her head, a declarative: I'm going to let you take me down. Apparently with Luke, she was more curious than usual.

Natasha was chewing on a cracker in a sliver of afternoon light that addressed the book shop window, when she finally fingered one of Luke's coffee table books off a tall shelf. She brought it to the worn chair and shooed the shop-cat away. The dedication...To my darling wife. Natasha turned the page. If sepia images of tack and shit stained boots could be stirring, his were. Natasha returned the sixty dollar book face out on the shelf. In actuality, Natasha found the company of artists untenable.

After a while, Natasha acquired a talent for asking things of Luke—things she didn't even want, really—that she knew he was either unwilling or incapable of providing. Over martinis in a dark bar miles and miles from the lights of the town where on opposite sides they lived, Luke would wax about the ranch an old friend reacquainted had offered him access to for fishing and Natasha would immediately, without any desire to be in a small boat, say: Take me.

It was important to Natasha that they remain equal in what they perceived they were sacrificing to see each other. But an equality there was imagined since Luke thought himself from that first night, and somewhat still, more virtuous than Natasha for his long-standing domestic arrangements and his summation that no matter what else Natasha was, she would always be one of those women who landed in his town on the run from something typical.

Typical, Natasha was not. And easy to define? Not until she herself stuck to one idea.

Luke on the other hand, thought he knew who he was: good son, more than competent husband, excellent father to two shining dean's list students enrolled at old schools, someone who was always on time for appointments. And he might have had an idea of who he was becoming: someone who worked up a sweat over a woman who was not his wife. Once and then again, until it was a regular symptom of the kind of mid-life experimentation he considered himself above. The kind of man who made sweeping statements that women would do well to ignore. Such as, in some distant time, I can see us together permanently. Or, there's the plan for a space in the juniper just for us two. And then not.

Men were allowed the audacity of contrary feelings. Women were just liars.

Natasha was often challenging and confrontational. And Luke was irritatingly reasonable. His mind was perfectly ordered in that way. On ordinary man—as Natasha's exceptionally intoxicated girl friend described Luke at a Russian vodka bar in New York City's lower east side during a weekend she flew in to visit and Luke followed to meet her. An ordinary man who could inexplicably break Natasha's heart with the way his mouth turned when in his western candor he'd tell her No. No. Simply and finally and enough to make Natasha's blood boil. His answers never satisfied either of them.

Luke said to Natasha, "I don't think you're used to not getting your way."

It was true. Natasha was used to getting her way. Natasha possessed the kind of abandon men rented movies to see. One afternoon in a Motel 2, Natasha absently stuck her finger into Luke and only further categorized herself as the kind of woman you had an affair with. Luke bore down. Maybe it was part of the risk of his going to be late for dinner; still ahead of him, a thirty mile drive home to the table. He put Natasha on her back, held her hands over her head and drove himself through her losing the condom inside of her. "My nasty girl," he said. And Natasha clamped down hard and made him come too soon for either of their tastes.

The arrangements had been made some months before Luke was to present an award to a contemporary—an occurrence commonplace enough that no one at home with Luke made a peep about being invited or not—that she and Luke arrive in Tucson two days ahead of time.

When she checked in after Luke, Natasha put her side of their adjoined rooms on her Visa. The three drinks she had before undressing didn't reach her head. That Astroglide glistened on his fingers and his chin was a short coming Natasha was not about to take responsibility for. Natasha had learned a kind of perceptiveness prescriptive to men like Luke, and applied a keen intuition to the quiet moments between a man and a woman when nothing and everything is said. She listened carefully to the posture of his receiving a pleasant sensation he had no desire to interrupt but that didn't go beyond his belt buckle. Natasha was not one to congratulate herself all the time, though later she enjoyed a hot shower and the act of dressing for the reception of artists both renowned and burgeoning.

Natasha hid behind her drink while she craned to see around the ballroom. By this time, the familiar sounds of Luke articulating at a podium and the almost imperceptible phony cock of his head made him unbearable.

When involved with someone else's man, you begin to wonder how much and exactly what you and your competition might agree on. Natasha had a weird affection for his soft, small hands that every once in a while showed signs of bitten cuticles, though she'd never once seen Luke with his fingers in his mouth. Luke complained like a woman. That was one thing Natasha didn't like. But in the end, Natasha desired Luke because something about him seemed unprecedented in her personal history. After all it wasn't about monogamy, it was about exploration.

Natasha guffawed in her glass, reached for her purse and left the ballroom, for some reason paying careful attention to the feel of her high heels sinking into the thick hotel carpet as she made her way to the empty atrium bar, and two hours later, up to the room.

Natasha had to call security. She had to hand off her oily martini glass to the man while she fished in her purse for some ID. "Was the adjoining door left open, Miss?"

"Yes. We came out his door together. I didn't realize the latch on my door to the hall was thrown."

Later still, Luke woke her from where she lay across one of the two beds in her unused room. "What are you doing in here?" he said. "Come home."

Luke and Natasha shared a bath with one or two candles and a bottle of Maker's Mark. The bourbon and the gurgle of the Jacuzzi tub made her absent. Luke splashed Natasha often.

But he wasn't feeling well. Food too late. Too much to drink. Luke was conditioned to apologize. In spite of this strengths, he thought I'm Sorry was how you treated a woman.

The next afternoon, Natasha followed Luke around to the back of the truck where he had opened the tail gate and was reaching in to a cooler. Inside were two four packs of Beam and Cola in a can. He popped the top of one and handed it to her.

"It comes in a can? How wonderful," Natasha said.

"Just about everything comes in a can."

Out of a lock box, Luke pulled out a spiffy Smith and Wesson 2214 and began loading a magazine.

"Guns and booze. Woo-hoo!" Natasha said slapping her thigh.

"And dirty sex," Luke said without looking up.

Natasha leaned against the dusty SUV and watched, with the addition of a few props, Luke change from person to character: the uniform of his Stetson, seeming longer in his stiff jeans in that particular way men could be, a white button down with its western yokes and razor creases; Natasha watched flashes of the rust and cream tooled leather of his custom boots through the cheat grass. Luke was much more complicated than the stereotypes that were always a tempting way for his publicists to describe him, particularly because of his tendency to take advantage of such a myth. And while Natasha knew he was world traveled, she for the moment tried to picture him anywhere else and failed.

"Watcha doing?" he asked. They were both relaxed in spite of the sleepless night they spent on opposite sides of the bed.

"Admiring the fashion," Natasha said. She felt perfectly safe with him out in the middle of nowhere with a gun and a can of Beam and Cola because as Luke made sure she didn't forget, he had something important to lose.

"Take a hold of this," Luke said handing her the gun.

Natasha did, and for a moment he wouldn't let go.

"Seems obvious, but bears mentioning," Luke said. "This is a loaded firearm. Don't point it at me."

She didn't. Hit every small target on the wide landscape Luke pointed to and then swung the gun low and squeezed the trigger. That was pretty much the end of the road for Luke and Natasha.

Luke had no idea what the perception of his waning interest in her would do to Natasha. Until she shot him. Then he had some idea there was a problem. But he didn't really get it. He couldn't piece it together. Though she ruined his right boot, Luke still said he cared deeply for her. And this, apparently was enough of a justification for the sin of his getting naked with her. It was his story. And it made Natasha think he didn't care to know her well at all. And this was a bit disappointing.

It is interesting that it doesn't take much for life to change. For a day to fill with things, even simple things, other than what had occupied it even a short time before. It was a month since Tucson and only a week now before Luke would be showing his work at a competing gallery in the square. There were fliers advertising the opening reception on every public notice board.

Instead of Luke's wife, it was his brother who Natasha met at his reception; a shorter, less affluent version of Luke. Though the three of them talked for some time, Natasha couldn't decide how close the brothers really were. She remembered Luke mentioning that his brother did something in the oil industry and that his father made trinkets in his garage. Natasha was not especially adept at drawing people out by way of small talk, so things remained unclear in an uncomfortable way. Natasha had a knack of looking right in a man's face that Luke's brother openly found flattering and made Luke scoff, but all the while it was Natasha's method of spotting strange movements or anticipating strategies.

Natasha admired the mahogany cane that was bearing most of Luke's weight. Luke waddled when he walked, and used the fact of his fancy cane to lean on Natasha as they neared a small print framed by a linen mat of greater mass than the print itself. A black and white photo of Natasha's bare flank hung beside a slightly longer shot of the insistent desert sun striking the quarter panel of a decomposing Ford Muskrat that had been all but taken over by Lechugilla.

"That's madness," Natasha said.

"Maybe, but I've perfected some plausible statement on it to cover my artistic ass."

Natasha couldn't decide which shot inspired the other. She was going to miss Luke's irony.

"I'm feeling bad," Luke said quietly.

"What are you feeling bad about?"

"This meeting seems more morose than I wanted it to be."

"That's on you."

"What happened with us?"

"You mean besides that I shot you?"

"Yes."

"You tell me."

"I can't sustain the intensity."

"Who said you had to?"

"I did. Things got a little regular. The sex became routine."

"Is that so?"

"Do you disagree?"

"I'll admit that I felt less inclined to please you when I sensed a shift in our symbiosis."

Luke gave her his look. Taken aback, but not surprised.

"At this stage of the game Mr. Brick, it's all about commerce, wouldn't you say?"

"You think like a man," Luke called after her.

"Why shouldn't I? Men tend to win."

The town square was small and the bar where Natasha could see him through the neon and the smoke was very near to where Luke was concluding his business with the gallery owner. He was the brightest star in the local sky, of course everything sold. Natasha need only carry her drink to the open door to catch his eye, which she did and was all she had to do, and had a bourbon and water waiting for him when he appeared beside her.

"Where have you two been? I haven't seen you in ages," the bartender said. Luke looked caught and caged. Natasha wanted to smack the stupid woman for ruining the perfectly unthreatening scene she'd managed to create, but she ignored this feeling of helplessness.

"Relax," Natasha said to Luke. "All she remembers is the color of your wallet. How's that foot, by the way?"

"Healing."

"Good for you. You will agree that in Tucson you were a total prick, right?"

"Look. In our better moments, of which there were many, I could believe that I could be with you the person who was invisible to my wife. The person she didn't want to know. Then I would have to behave in a way that would perpetuate the funds with which I have created a life with my family or I would review all that would have to change and it would seem impossible for us to be together. So what it means is that, you shot me, and I will have to forget you. Which I started to do. But it's taken longer than I thought."

"You are something. Do you think that's it?"

"Yes." He made his 'you're an idiot' face. Natasha motioned for a refill.

"What it amounts to, I suppose, is that all I could offer you is the fact that I love you. Which I do."

"Oh, there wasn't a moment in there somewhere when you were hoping I'd ask you to leave home, and then another moment when you were terribly relieved to know that I would never ask?"

"Yes."

"How indulgent."

"Yes."

"I envy you."

On Being Misidentified

It was the kind of bar that was full of aching backs and broken hearts. Natasha got excited when she pulled up and even more so when she pushed open the door and that distinctive waft of whiskey and sweat grabbed her by the hair.

The game was on with no sound and from a back room came the smack of a successful break. Natasha loved bars like these. She knew that her red lipstick would eventually make some hopeful sucker want to buy her a round. And then what? The point was not the drink, the point was that moment when one smile would say that he'd misjudged Natasha completely. Or maybe, not.

Holding a short glass with two fingers of Beam in his hand and in no particular hurry, Jim rounded the horseshoe of the bar to reach Natasha. Jim smelled clean, like the Pantene shampoo samples that were sink-side in the empty rooms where he napped between shows, between cities, mostly in a different one every day now that he was a less famous musician. Though even when Jim was clean—even slightly pink from a hot shower—dressed in pressed clothes and his heavy gold watch, there was a note of whiskey.

Jim kissed Natasha on the mouth and pat at his chest for something he could not find. Jim still thought himself wild and unattached, but he was a creature of habit. He liked things to happen at precise, recurring times, in precise recurring ways. Apparently it was perfectly reasonable for Natasha to be sitting in Jim's regular seat at his favorite bar, two states away from where she lived.

Tim the bartender, with his seen-it-all look on his face, squeaked a rag in the hollow of a glass.

"Three months on the road and where else would I have found him on his first night home, refrigerator empty of ice. I, on the other hand, have this distaste for being identified," Natasha said, leaning an elbow on the bar to adjust her skirt.

Tim slid the glass into the rack over his head where some like it were hanging. "Is that all?"

"What do cigarettes cost now? Seven dollars?" Jim shook a Kool loose from a tight pack, slid it all the way out with his mouth. "Ever notice how you can leave a drink and a full pack of cigarettes on a bar and it's the fifty cent Bic lighter that'll walk away?"

Tim snapped a match for him. Jim said, "You remember Tim, don't you Natasha?"

"How could I forget."

"You remember Natasha, don't you Tim?"

"Not until I saw you walk in. And then I remembered."

"You fake it well," Natasha said.

"It's his job," Jim said.

Natasha drinks and thinks about the days after she had last seen Jim. It was real, even though it seemed like sleep walking. There's always the smell of him when the glass of Jim Beam and Coke fit under her nose, *Rubber Soul* reliably on the jukebox and loose cigarettes to be smoked. And how can she not think of Jim.

Jim had said love before; he had been twenty-nine and Natasha was nineteen. And after that, peppered with other likely confessions of devotion aggressive sex makes rise to the surface.

Then it was a stand alone profession; a message left on a voice mail after a lot of time and space and baggage had accumulated. Natasha was thirty and Jim forty. I miss you. I love you. And Natasha would feel like replying.

"You can tell just by the plate how good the burger is," Jim advised as Tom slapped a cheese burger deluxe in front of him. "I think musicians make bad husbands," Jim said swallowing.

"Do you?" Natasha asked. "I think too good a husband makes a dishonest wife." Natasha put down her empty glass.

"Is that so?"

"Well some women are best suited to men they can't tame. Nothing else satisfies. Oh, I love this song," Natasha swivelled her stool to see who was standing at the juke box. "Don't look at me like I have two heads!" she laughed.

"No, no. This is very interesting."

"I figure, better to understand your definition and wear it like a diamond tiara."

"Go on."

"Well, OK, you rock stars are all the same. You're all drunk, high, and unavailable. You leave home anxious and over-excited and come back full of either self-pity or self-congratulation."

"Well if that's not stereotyping."

"Oh, like I'm not stereotyped?" Natasha said.

"Never mind."

Natasha hopped off the stool. "I really love this song. Come dance with me."

Jim dropped his cigarette in an ashtray and followed Natasha onto the parquet. He wrapped Natasha up and she disappeared. "You have some interesting theories," he said.

"A musician is a fine man. He inspires love. Here, here. This is my favorite part." I stopped moving with him. "'...oh, but she can't take you any way, you don't already know how to go.'"

When she'd been sleeping at Jim's house last, he gave her a bloody nose. The night before Natasha left. Two years ago. He never knew. Night terrors.

Some days Jim has memory and others not. It's not a break in synapse; it's chosen. Jim can remember the name on the tag beside the dress zipper he yanked open at the wheel of his leased Dodge truck in the parking lot of this bar, but how long it's been, exactly since he's seen Natasha last? Not sure. Did it matter?

"I called your house once or twice Natasha," Jim said. "Some guy answered. Was your dad visiting?"

Natasha and Jim will have sex, but they won't discuss that she's there.

RoseMarie

Red, Blue and the WWE

You probably didn't notice me, but I was in New York City a while back. I drove two and a half hours from a small town in Wyoming to Denver International Airport where I bought some fashion magazines and sat at the gate to wait for my flight. While flipping through *Jane*, a man and a woman—colleagues forced into the intimacy of a business trip—sat down across from me a seat apart. The man handed the woman one of the two bottles of Artesian water he'd purchased. A thoughtfulness to which his travel companion replied, "I can't drink that. I only drink Poland Springs. Did you see any Poland Springs?" The man didn't answer.

I was on my way to New York City to meet the professional wrestler Triple H who was on a press junket for his new movie *Blade Trinity* and was doing a signing at the Virgin Megastore to promote his body building book *Making the Game*. My fixation for Triple H took even me by surprise and corresponded with a

prescription for Prozac for the low grade anxiety that had mani-
fested since I slowed down to a small town pace.

Somehow, Monday Night RAW, the flagship of World
Wrestling Entertainment's many broadcast shows, had become a
standing date for me and my boyfriend Jeff whose own wrestling
fandom began as a boy in his parents' basement in Michigan
back in the days of Georgia Championship. Every week we meet
at home just before seven, close the blinds and gorge ourselves
on Mexican food in front of the TV. And now and then on a
Tuesday morning I'd forward my friend Amy, a senior editor at
Simon and Schuster, links to especially sweaty Triple H photos
from the WWE website as a gag. And once in a while to my
delight Amy would reply, "Is that *blood?*"

Amy and I met when we both worked at Little, Brown and
Company and have managed to keep in touch in spite of the fact
I left my native New York for a Red State where I can drink
whiskey all night with less than ten dollars in my pocket.
Actually, Amy's been out to visit, once or twice during Jubilee
Days where she watched most of the Mr. T. Classic Bullriding
out at the fairgrounds through her fingers.

When the WWE came to Laramie, Jeff managed to catch me
by the scruff of the neck when in my unchecked excitement I
almost went ass-over-tea-kettle down the University of
Wyoming Arena stairs. Stripped of my big-city pretension, I
confess I enjoyed being mocked by a shake-and-baked, over
developed—albeit beautiful—circus-freak who shouted that we
women in the audience looked like buffaloes and our male com-
panions buffalo farmers. I glanced around me and didn't see anyone I knew from the independent bookstore that I managed, or
the intellectual circles in which I run. The Arena was populated
by some underground Laramie society I'd never seen and perhaps
Triple H's insult was not that far off. If there was any discomfort
in this, it was short lived as according to what Walter Kirn
wrote recently for the *New York Times Book Review*, it is me in all

of my "Red State, fly-fishing, NASCAR loving, God-fearing ruralness," who is the new Urban Sophisticate.

"There is this whole theory," a Laramie friend says of my interest in Triple H. "That part of sexual attraction is governed by certain genes wanting to perpetuate themselves." This friend works for the EPA and majored in neuroscience. She likes to play with bats. "You are just a neanderthal in Kate Spade sunglasses, which is why you like to watch him. Backward genes longing to combine again."

"That must explain why I fell down the stairs," I said. "Backward genes attempting to recombine can't be good for one's motor skills."

I landed at LaGuardia at 10:30 p.m. and was immediately in a familiar rush to find a cab to the Flatiron Lounge where Amy and a perfect martini were waiting for me. And first thing in the morning I was standing in a seventeenth floor conference room in Rockefeller Center staring at how Triple H could not close his thighs beneath the table.

I knew of course that Paul Levesque the man, was not Triple H. That Triple H, the "franchise player" was a fiction. And yet, my backward genes had longed to meet the character. Swaggering and large. Roaring, shimmering with sweat and full of threat. Instead, I got cashmere.

Later, Amy and I were having cocktails at Double Happiness with two women she'd met networking through New York City's Young Women in Media who were both dying to hear about the day.

"Amy and I were the first to arrive," I said. "And when we left, the line to get in wrapped around the corner and back to the elevator."

"You're kidding me?" one said.

"Yes. I was amazed," Amy said.

"At what? It's Triple H!," I said.

"I think it's hilarious that you applied for an artist's grant to come here," one said. "Amy forwarded me what you wrote on your application. It was very well spun. No wonder you got it."

I put a hand over my heart. "Why, thank you." I had to shout; *King of the Night Time World* blared from a speaker over top of us.

"I was sure she wouldn't keep her shit together," Amy said. "But she was very calm."

"Well, I was totally thrown off by the expensive chartreuse sweater he was wearing. Where was all the anger? Where was the blood?" I said. "Oh, but I did get to rest my cheek on his great big shoulder when Amy took our picture," I said touching the side of my face.

"Yeah, I'm the bomb," Amy said. "She asks me for a book, I provide the man."

The next afternoon I was off to a lunch appointment to pitch a novel I'd recently completed while in residence at the Ucross Foundation. I waited for Sarah, the editor I worked for before leaving the City who now had her own Imprint, outside the Union Square Café in plain sight of the Virgin Megastore and one of my favorite shoe stores.

The dining room teemed with publishing folk sitting at their regular tables and I followed Sarah to hers. Over the artful design of spicy lamb sausage and cold curried carrots on my plate, I spoke of my writing with enthusiastic gesticulations and bursts of loud description that I thought might serve me well.

I told Sarah of my taste for fresh game meat, my penchant for the inappropriate sport of Rodeo and a little bit about how wonderful Wyoming truly is. "A couple of days ago, just about at dusk, my friend Mike and I drove about fifteen minutes north of town with the frozen hide of a two year old buffalo cow in the bed of his tricked out Chevy Silverado. Someone Mike works with went on one of those organized bow and arrow Buffalo hunts. Mike had dibs on the hide and he's getting it tanned for my birthday. Mike and I kept having to stop and open gates to get to the taxidermist guy's ranch. The sunset was glorious and the snow on the prairie was blue and we only laughed when it was discovered that the truck's four wheel drive is out. I thought, I could live out of town. I could write about this. I could live out of the city limits, making cow-eyes at the cows through the window. At least I think I could.

"But," I said, leaning over my plate towards the woman who, as a going away gift, gave me a fifty dollar gift certificate to Sephora so that I might stave off the evils of drug store lipstick at least for a while. "Can I tell you why I've come back?"

"Something tremendous, one would have to assume," Sarah said.

"In a way, yes. I flew in yesterday to meet the Wrestling Superstar Triple H. He's just published a body building book. You remember Amy, don't you? She cornered his publicist in some hallway and arranged my VIP status for his book signing tonight.

"The best part is that you know I will end up writing about it. So after I booked my flight, I applied for an individual artist grant and now the whole fantasy is being supported in part by the Wyoming Arts Council. As a condition of the award, I am required to say that."

"I don't believe it," Sarah laughed. "It's a perfect story for the op-ed page in the *Times*."

"I see what you mean. How this former Blue State Girl moves to a Red State, uses a Blue State method, i.e. a government grant, to travel back to her native Blue State to meet a Red State kind of guy and then goes back to her Red State to write the essay about how she's able to work both the Blue and the Red State systems. I'm a straddler."

At coat check, I gave someone a few dollars to get my electric blue Persian lamb and silver mink fur collared coat back.

"Where on earth did you find that?" Sarah asked.

"In a consignment shop in Laramie. Can you imagine?" I held it open to show her the immaculate lining. "It's never been worn."

"In Laramie?" Sarah said. "You certainly seem to be thriving there."

"Yeah, the leanings of this Administration have afforded some cultural clout to all of my backwoods amusements," I told Sarah. "And so with some new legitimacy I get to jet to New York to meet a professional wrestler from the WWE and have a delicious power-lunch with my former boss. But they've yet to get me back into Church."

Author's Note:

Contact the author at RM_London@hotmail.com

978-0-595-35754-3
0-595-35754-7

Printed in the United States
36056LVS00002BA/130-132

9 780595 357543